NEVER LOOK BACK

Nina, anxious to save her marriage to Charles, wants to stop the rot before it's too late. Charles, refusing to admit that there is anything wrong, tells Nina to stop imagining problems. But there is her step-brother, Duncan Stevens — easy-going and artistic, everything that Charles is not . . . Charles' sister-in-law likens divorce to a mere game of chess — yet the effect of a tragic death, seven years previously, triggers off a happening of such magnitude that Nina faces the truth at last.

JANET ROSCOE

NEVER
LOOK BACK

Complete and Unabridged

LINFORD
Leicester

First published in Great Britain in 1974 by
Robert Hale & Company
London

First Linford Edition
published 2008
by arrangement with
Robert Hale Limited
London

British Library CIP Data

Roscoe, Janet
Never look back.—Large print ed.—
Linford romance library
1. Love stories
2. Large type books
I. Title
823.9'14 [F]

ISBN 978–1–84782–264–2

Published by
F. A. Thorpe (Publishing)
Anstey, Leicestershire

Set by Words & Graphics Ltd.
Anstey, Leicestershire
Printed and bound in Great Britain by
T. J. International Ltd., Padstow, Cornwall

This book is printed on acid-free paper

1

'Charles keeping well Nina?' Mr. Fenner unhooked the drill from its stand and straddled his little round stool.

I managed an unintelligible 'yes' from the depths of my throat seconds before the drill snarled into my tooth. Oh how I hate having teeth filled! How I hate it, hate it, hate it! I hate the whole business of going to the dentist's . . . the huge hand, the hovering face, and that ghastly drill, biting and gnawing, grrr-ing and garrr-ing, exploding one's head with noise. And the fearsome thoughts that run rampant at such times: supposing he drops it, supposing he lets it slip, supposing it eats its way right through my cheek, or flips up through the roof of my mouth.

Would Charles notice if I had a hole in my face, were dreadfully scarred for life? Of course he would, he'd be very upset, but I mustn't keep thinking of Charles. Was he regretting that we'd ever linked up, could I be feeling the same? But these were traitorous, awful, disloyal thoughts. We were married, legally bound, we'd got to make it work. And it was silly to worry. It was only a phase. Most marriages went through a period of doldrums. In time we'd sail out of ours.

The drill was insistent. I couldn't think of Charles . . . vibrating and jarring, digging down deep . . . a hot smell, a charred odour, flying bits and panic, feeling clamped in the chair. Oh can't he stop, can't he stop, he must have finished now . . . until with a final cacophony of sound it was out of my mouth at last, whirring harmlessly in the air, like a bumble bee buzzing against glass.

'Rinse please.'

The cavity felt enormous. I explored it with my tongue. Need he have churned out quite as much as that? It didn't feel like my tooth at all. And then the plastic strips, the pads of gauze, the hooked-over waterdrain thing. He was packing my tooth now, moving in close, his breath a soft tickle through the mask. He smiled at me above it, his cheeks broadening out. He had the same kind of wiry hair as Charles, in the same dark chestnut brown.

'Your mouth's in very good shape, young lady. If all my patients had teeth like yours I'd be out of business by the end of the year. Charles is all right you say?'

'Yes, he's fine, thank you.'

'Seems a long time since you two were living over the surgery here. How long is it — six months?'

'You're way out Mr. Fenner. It's two whole years!'

'Two years! As long at that? Well bless my soul!'

He removed the strips and the gauze, unhooked the drain from my jaw, and asked me to close my teeth down. This I did gingerly, wary of the crunch, and he smiled at me encouragingly again.

'Like your house in The Drive?'

'Very much.' (But I don't, I hate it. Why keep pretending, why not speak the truth for once?)

Mr. Fenner grunted as he smeared my teeth with paste and fitted another gadget on the drill. Knowing he'd only polish now I prepared to relax, staring over his shoulder at the station buildings opposite, and thinking of days gone by.

When Charles and I were first married, four years ago, we'd had the flat over Mr. Fenner's surgery. Lonely during the day I'd looked forward to the evening, when I could sit in the window and watch the commuter trains arrive, spilling out their crowds on the 'down' side platform, then humming on again towards Redhill and the south. We'd been very much in love then. My heart would begin to thunder in my chest, the blood flow warm in my veins. Charles would be somewhere in that shifting mass of people, swarming over

4

the iron bridge like flies.

As soon as he emerged from the booking-hall I'd see him. He'd look up and wave, crossing the road at the lights, the evening paper and his zip-up briefcase bundled under one arm. He was fantastically good-looking, he stood out from other men, with that tall lean body and thrusting wedge of face, pale under the well-groomed thatch of thick dark red hair.

Charles Edward Redman ... he'd swept me off my feet; he'd captured and captivated me, blinded me to all else, and he'd come along at just at the right time. But time changes things and people, and Charles and I had changed. We'd sobered down, we'd flattened out, our feelings were no longer knife-keen.

Of course no one can expect to live at bliss level, not the absolute whole of life through, but there should be liberal patches of it, little oases, just to confirm one is on the right lines. And I didn't know now, I just didn't know; it was like stumbling about in the dark. All I did know was we habitually bickered, and when I suggested something might be going wrong, Charles flew into a paddy (red-haired men often do) and told me I expected too much. Perhaps I did; he could be right; it was very possible of course. It was also just possible that we hadn't begun right, hadn't built our foundations on rock-firm ground, hadn't looked below the surface at the start.

Marriage, they say, is always a gamble, but ours had had especial hazards in that we'd met and married within only six weeks, knowing very little about each other at all. It had been at a mutually crucial time, a vulnerable time for us both. Charles had been getting over an abortive love affair, and I'd been unsettled and ready to leap after father married again. I'd been in love with Charles, of course; nothing and no one and no kind of circumstance would have prompted me to marry him if I hadn't felt that way, but I think perhaps on his side, taking a long cool look back, he could have been rebounding and trying to fill the gap left by the other girl he'd loved. He'd never told me anything about that girl, 'Pointless to rehash,' he'd said.

And even during the first year, even at our zenith, I knew I wasn't the ideal wife for Charles. He was serious-minded and my airiness irked him, especially over things which he thought mattered and which to me had no significance at all. It soon became obvious that he was very ambitious and I'm afraid I hadn't realised that before; all that striving and straining, cultivating the right people, it didn't seem worth it to me. But I was nevertheless terrifically pleased and very, very proud, when after we'd been married exactly two years, he was offered a partnership in his firm. The firm was Rudgleys Solicitors of Norfolk Street, The Strand, and even I in my ignorance knew it was an honour to be asked to join their ranks at only thirty years of age.

Again looking back though, I think it was roughly then that the first 'wind of change' began to blow — a change that was to make us less aware of one another, to set us, as it were, on separate paths.

Soon after our move into No. 5 The Drive, I became pregnant with Sue. This made a difference, we both wanted children, it seemed too good to be true. It also, I thought, was a very happy omen, surely all the gods were on our side. But they weren't, or one wasn't, maybe none of them were, for I miscarried my baby at four and a half months, after a virulent attack of 'flu.

I felt changed afterwards. I didn't feel like me. I couldn't turn to anyone, not even Charles. I just wanted to be by myself.

'We'll have another darling . . . ' (this was Charles, all haggard-eyed) . . . 'we'll have another; you're very young; try not to brood on it any more.'

I tried, but I couldn't rouse, I felt

quite dead inside. And everyone was determined to cheer me up.

'Start another,' advised our doctor, when I came out of hospital . . . 'give yourself six months and off you go again,' . . . as though I were planning to sail round the world, or try my hand at walking on the moon.

I know they meant to be kind and they were probably quite right, but what I couldn't get over to them, couldn't explain, was that I'd never have *that* baby, I'd never have Sue . . . the child whom I'd longed for, given identity in my mind, pictured her as she'd lie in my arms. Couldn't they understand that, couldn't they *see* . . . however many children I had in the future, I'd never have the one that had gone. This was eighteen months ago and I'd never conceived again, so perhaps I wasn't meant to have a child.

Mr. Fenner moved away from me, jerking at my bib.

'Well, there you are my dear. That's it for another six months. And don't forget to remind Charles about his appointment on the eighth; it's a Saturday morning, special concession for him!'

I thanked him as profusely as my stretched face would allow, and paying my money in the adjoining small office, clattered down the stairs to the street.

I shivered as the brown door banged behind me. It was the end of March, the beginning of spring, the tail end of a winter that still struck very chill. I turned up the collar of my new suede coat and set off briskly for home. The long cheval mirror in Merrick's furniture shop showed a tall thin girl with straight black hair that lifted up untidily in the wind. To be honest I quite like being tall and thin, because I can wear trendy clothes in stark bold designs, and whatever sort of colour is in vogue. 'My Romany Nina', Charles used to call me. I'm like my mother, or like my mother was. She died seven years ago when I was just seventeen.

I quickened my pace as I felt the first

drops of rain. I didn't want my coat to get wet. I was passing the houses at the bottom of The Drive . . . 'The Larches', 'The Limes', 'The Cedars', 'The Elms'. Ours had been 'The Beeches', but Charles changed it to 'High Walls'. It certainly lived up to its name.

The gates, which were iron, were the same height as the walls, and looked like those of a hospital, or school, or prison, or cemetery, depending on one's mood. I opened them, clanged them to, made my way up the drive, my heels sinking soggily in the newly raked path.

The garden looked untidy after the heavy spring rains. The daffodils had keeled over so that their trumpets touched the ground, their foliage lay like laces on the lawn. I'd have to cut them and mass them indoors. It was a shame to let them bruise in the wind.

I loved the garden. It wasn't too big for me to manage on my own, and Charles didn't mind me taking it over. He mowed the lawns and pruned the trees and cut the beech hedge, but he never interfered with the planning and planting, and he let me do as I pleased. The garden had been a great solace, ever since Sue. In a very different way, of course, I was creating something again, and I think Charles understood this and let me have free rein.

But try as I might I couldn't like the house. It was dismal and aloof, mock-Tudor and ornate, and although the windows were numerous they were also very small, they never seemed to yield enough light. So there it was . . . a mausoleum of a house, but it had been given to us (literally) by Sir William (Charles' father) which meant that we'd got it for life.

I went down the sideway and unlocked the back door, stepping into the warmth of the large square kitchen, which was the friendliest room in the house. Here I heated some coffee and cut a piece of cake, eating it up at the breakfast bar, wary of my newly filled tooth. I twisted my legs round the stem of the stool, drinking my coffee from a mug. I like to be informal, to let my hair down ... to go back if only momentarily to my pre-marriage days, when I'd run around gaily with 'the crowd'; a harmless enough crowd, but we'd had a lot of fun. It seemed a long time ago now.

Charles wasn't fond of eating in the kitchen. He liked a well laid table, he said. I suppose, to be honest, and in the nicest possible way, some people would call him a snob. He's not one of the hoity sort, he doesn't look down on people, or anything like that, but he's very conscious indeed of family and background, and he does tend to categorise a lot. This is only natural, because it's the way he's been brought up, but it does make for arguments at times.

I'm fond of my in-laws, though. They're all very nice. Sir William is nearly eighty and has a weak heart; there's Uncle Joscelyn (his brother) who's something big in tea; there's Tim

(Charles' brother) who's a chartered accountant, and there's Dallas (Tim's wife) who's Hungarian-born and gorgeous and leads Tim a bit of a dance.

Bearing in mind his position with Rudgleys, Charles says it's vital that we socialise freely, are seen to be going around. So we give parties and go to parties and do our social thing, and we keep smiling rigidly all the time. Charles is a charmer, is naturally sociable. I have to force myself on.

'I'm dead on my feet Charles — that terrible old man!'

'I know he's a crashing bore, but he's loaded and influential. He could bring a lot of business to the firm.'

Conscious of failure I'd be apt to snap back. 'I should have thought the mighty Rudgleys had enough business already, with contacts to maintain the flow!'

'My efforts being 'coals to Newcastle', I suppose?'

'I didn't mean that.'

'It sounded very much like it. You

14

know as well as I do that lawyers can't tout. They have to be wily and try to attract work. That's what I'm trying to do.'

'Yes I know, I'm sorry Charles. I'll try harder next time.'

And I did try but it was no good, I didn't go over well, and in my heart of hearts I thought I knew why. Despite my fervent efforts I was a rotten actress, and these so-called new friends of ours weren't fools. Vain they might be, but foolish never; they saw through me all right. They recognised my tongue-in-cheek for precisely what it was, and they gave me a pretty wide berth.

Charles never complained. He said he liked me as I was, but I had a guilty feeling that I'd let him down again.

And just lately, these last few months, things had gone from bad to worse. Our bickerings had become arguments, our arguments full-scale rows. They weren't the sort of rows, moreover, that are supposed to clear the air. They just left nasty jagged scars.

Once in the dead of night, lying wakeful by Charles' side, I'd wondered if he'd ceased to care, had fallen for someone else. The thought was painful, wounding, yet possible too, yet I turned it down out-of-hand. Charles was decent, open, disconcertingly honest, he wouldn't cheat me like that. But perhaps it had happened and he was fighting against it; that might account for his moods. And as I lay there stiff and miserable, my nose an inch from his back, the words of a schoolfriend came back to mind; 'I don't care if my husband *is* unfaithful to me, so long as he doesn't tell me about it.' How head-in-the-sand, what rubbish, I'd thought, what a puerile, ineffectual thing to say, for if one had a normal marital relationship how could one *fail* to know.

And Charles and I did have a normal relationship. It was only just a little blunted down.

★　★　★

He got home later than usual that evening. It was dusk when at last he came striding up the drive, a light belted raincoat over his suit. It was still raining thickly and he had an old black hat perched a little rakishly on his head.

'Hullo,' he said, as he stepped into the hall, 'how did you get on with old Fenner?'

'All right.' We kissed but didn't look each other properly in the eye. We'd had an argument over breakfast and embarrassment remained. It couldn't be blotted out at once.

'Had a good day?' I took his raincoat from him and hung it by the radiator, stealing a glance at his face.

'Not bad. I've got something to talk over with you, but I'll get changed first. I feel like a trussed up turkey in this suit.'

He made for the stairs taking them two at a time. I stood there on the hall mat.

'Talk about what, Charles? Is it nice or nasty?'

'Depends on how you look at it.' His voice came, faintly muffled now, from the direction of the bedroom, 'I'll be down in a second. Let's have a sherry — some of that medium dry.'

I took the drinks into the sitting-room and switched on the fire, watching the light revolve behind the 'coals'. What did he mean? What sort of a talk? Was it going to mean a change? Was it something at work? Did it affect the two of us, he and me? My tooth began to throb, my mouth went dry. Was it something serious? Was he fed up with the rows? Supposing he wanted to be free. But this was silly, we were married, we'd got to see it through; it wasn't something little that could be lightly tossed aside. But my hands shook nervously and I gripped them tight together. How dreadful to feel as uncertain as this . . . uncertain, unsafe, insecure.

Perhaps we shouldn't have married, merely shacked-up together, been modern and way-out, just living for the day.

How would it have been if we'd merely lived together — no marriage vows to keep, no worry not having a child, no artificial friends and colleagues, no dull formal clothes. And I could have had a job, any job I liked. I wouldn't have had to obey Charles, do as he decreed. It was about my taking a job that we'd quarrelled this morning. I did so want to have one and he was all against it, 'It's simply not necessary,' he'd said. But it *was* necessary to me, I'd got to do something, I couldn't just exist like some sort of backcloth, nothing but a stay-at-home wife.

Charles came down in his yellow cashmere sweater and the fawn denim trousers he wore at weekends. His face seemed to me to be paler than usual, his freckles showed up plainly on his nose. He flopped down in the leather armchair and swallowed his sherry in one.

'That was quick!'

'I know, but I needed it. Nina, listen, how would you like to live on the coast again . . . good old Sussex by the sea?'

'On the *coast*!'

'Sussex darling, rolling Downs, grazing sheep, high winds . . . the lot!'

'Are you . . . is it . . . are you joking?'

'No.' His mouth was taking on its lopsided look, which meant he was thinking hard. A faint sort of hope began to curl up within me. Were we moving . . . starting afresh . . . had something happened?

'For goodness sake tell me, or I shall absolutely *burst*!'

'Rudgleys are thinking of opening a branch office in Brighton. They want me to take sole charge.'

'Oh Charles . . . oh Charles . . . oh darling . . . how marvellous!' My sherry flip-flopped in my glass.

'Steady now darling. Don't get too excited. It's all in embryo stage, there's nothing definitely settled. But what I thought was . . . well how would you feel about it if it did come off? Would you like to live down there again?'

'I'd adore it . . . it'd be super . . . it'd

20

be absolute bliss!' And it would, of course, it would, it would. To move away, leave Cranston Heath, leave this house, start afresh. And he'd asked me, he'd asked me, he minded what I felt . . . that to me meant more than anything else, so . . . 'Oh Charles . . . oh Charles . . . ' was all I could manage and my sherry tipped on to the floor.

'You mad creature!' He came over and kissed me and mopped up the mess, his head bent over his task. I touched his hair gently, feeling it rise under my hand. Dear Charles . . . dear Charles . . . he was so much nicer than me . . . there was so much to look up to and admire.

'But will it happen? Will it really happen? And when will we move? Will we sell this house and will Sir William mind?'

'I don't know yet, to all those questions. We'll have to wait and see.'

'Would it be a step up for you?'

'I'm not sure.' He poured me another sherry and filled his own glass, walking with it over to the uncurtained window, staring a little moodily outside. 'There'd be nothing much in it financially better, but I wouldn't mind that because I'd have more scope.' He pulled the cord at the window and the curtains slid to . . . orange-gold velvet, expensively lined, just a shade lighter than the russet pile carpet which we'd had laid down last year; trappings, just trappings, the outward signs of success; I liked them, but I could do without them, they were almost *too* lush. Oh Charles come and sit down, talk to me properly, don't just keep walking up and down. He did so, so suddenly that I wondered for a moment if my thoughts had transmitted themselves audibly through the air.

'It would be the old, old story of a big frog in a little puddle!' He gave his crooked smile as he sprawled in the chair, holding out his hand to me. 'And in Town I'm a very wee froggie indeed, almost a tadpole in fact!'

'I don't believe it!' I sprang up and sat on the arm of his chair; his hand curled about my waist, 'Anyway in Brighton it'd be different, you'd be a *huge* frog, and Brighton isn't a litle puddle it's a great big thriving town. Not only that but Sussex is full of wealthy people, writers and actors and artists and all that. They're always in messes, always wanting advice. Rudgleys would make a bomb down there.'

'They'd have plenty of competition. There are nearly as many legal offices in Brighton as oil-bespattered pebbles on the beach.'

'Rudgleys could stand it, think of their fame. And lots of their clients must live down there already; a local office would save them trekking to Town.'

'Clever Neenie!' The pet name slipped out, and I turned round and kissed him, suddenly charged with hope. This was all we needed, a brand new start, a new start away from this hemmed-in existence, and Charles and I would find each other again.

'But you lived at Fawding, didn't

you?' He pulled me on to his lap, and I leaned against his shoulder, my forehead touching his neck.

'Yes, but we used to go into Brighton quite a lot, you know. Mother bought her clothes there, and she was mad about antiques, and we always had our lunch in The Lanes. Oh Charles it's a super place, gay and raffish, cosmopolitan and rough, but you can be *real* there, you can let go, you don't have to pretend. I hope we can live there, oh I do hope we can!'

'Well the wind seems to be blowing in that direction at the moment.' His lips brushed my face, travelled down to my throat, whilst a great tide of warmth charged through my body, stirring me to life again. It was so simple . . . it was there . . . why did we lose touch . . . why did we lose touch and closeness slip away?

'Charles . . . '

'Mm . . . '

'You've got to like it too, you know, moving to Brighton I mean. It's very different from here, less formal, less ordered, less tidy too in a way. I'd adore it, of course, it's definitely my scene, but it has to be what you want in the end. I wouldn't want it if you didn't, that's what I'm trying to say.'

'I do have a choice.' He shifted in his chair and I went back to mine; the fleeting moment of unity had gone, 'Even if Rudgleys get the premises they want, I can still please myself whether I go there or not. They've put it to me on those terms.'

'Whatever you decide it's all right by me. I'd like to go to Brighton, but so long as things are all right between us, I don't care a damn either way.'

I'd said the wrong thing. I saw his head jerk up. 'What do you mean . . . so long as things are all right between us?'

'So long as we're happy together.'

'Well who's querying that for God's sake!' His anger ignited mine, I fought to keep calm, to say what I had to say.

'You've been worried and off-beat Charles . . . you know that you have. It hasn't exactly made for harmony between us. I'm your wife, I want to help, I want to know what it is, I don't want to be left in the dark!'

'Oh, for crying out loud!' He sprang to his feet, arms stiff at his sides, the lines round his mouth sharply etched. 'Once and for all, Janina, I am *not* worried, there's nothing wrong, there's not going to be anything *go* wrong. So stop imagining things and situations that simply don't exist!'

'Charles!'

'And I wish you wouldn't watch me around all the while as though you're expecting me to lay some ruddy egg!'

'Charles!'

'It's demoralising, I tell you . . . makes me feel caged!'

'What a horrible thing to say!'

'It's the way I feel, so drop it, *please*!'

I was suddenly so angry I couldn't say a word. I turned and stumbled over to the door.

'Nina . . .'

'I'm going to get supper. I shall be

half an hour.' I managed just before my voice broke.

In the kitchen I wept the hot tears of fury. I was angry resentful, hurt. I'd been side-tracked again, shoved away, fobbed off. There *was* something worrying him; he was keeping it to himself. It was all so ridiculous, I *wanted* to share, that's what loving a man meant. But perhaps he didn't love me, perhaps he didn't trust me, perhaps, if the truth be known, he'd like to push me out of his life. But he couldn't, we were married, for better, for worse. Well, so what, who cared, they were soppy words anyway. I mopped up my face, tipped coffee into the percolator, and got the chops out of the fridge. And gradually as I set about doing these ordinary tasks, a lot of the sore feeling seemed to ease away. It could be that I didn't care as much as I thought I did. Perhaps I was growing another skin. There are degrees of caring too, and the stark truth was I didn't care as much about being snubbed by Charles as I would have done three years ago when I'd still been fathoms deep. Yes, that was it, of course . . . you can be mortally wounded when you care deeply, when you care less it's easier, when you care scarcely at all it's a piece of cake . . . nothing much touches you any more. So perhaps that was the crux of the trouble between us. Independence was sifting through our marriage fortress now — a heady independence and a dangerous one too, for we'd lost the urge to turn to one another. In the things that really mattered we no longer clung hard. We were seldom impelled to share.

We made up the quarrel, of course; we were neither of us prone to sulks, but the scar remained, the damage was done, we'd only papered over the cracks.

2

Primroses dotted the railway banks, sprung up in clumps in the thick tussocky grass. Under the newly leafing trees in the coppices and spinneys I fancied I could glimpse a haze of blue. Bluebells, I thought, with a sigh of pleasure, just before the train plunged into the tunnel uttering an eldritch shriek.

The lights flicked on in the half-empty compartment, which was the sort with a corridor down the middle. It rocked as it hurtled through the dank-smelling tunnel. It was running about ten minutes late. Not that it mattered, of course. It was enough for me that I was actually in it, going down to Brighton, and from Brighton to Fawding, for the first time ever since mother had died.

I'd been born in Fawding, done my growing-up there, and it was a strange feeling to be going back, a little frightening too. I wanted to go, I had to visit the place, yet I dreaded the first awful plunge. And it was essential that I did plunge. I'd got to lay this ghost. I'd told Charles I wanted to live there, or at any rate at Brighton, so I'd got to get rid of my fear of the past or fear that the past might intrude.

Fawding is about eight miles from Brighton and lies on its eastern side. There are really three parts of it. Fawding town (old, tiny and picturesque), Fawding bay (the bathing and holiday part) and last but not least the magnificent roll of cliffs, which rise at one point to well over three hundred feet, this part being called Fawding Head.

We'd lived at the eastern end of the town. Father had been the local doctor, so everyone knew us well. But Fawding had become a nightmare place after mother died. Father had given up the practice and taken another in Lemston, Norfolk, less than three months after her death. I'd just left school and of course I'd gone with him, but I'd never forgotten the horror of that time, nor how father had aged overnight.

Yet it was seven years ago now, seven whole years . . . a long time, practically a decade. Father had married again, so he must have got over it. I had too, but there were nevertheless times when my thoughts went back to that day in October when the police had come to the door. What had happened that day . . . what really *had* happened . . . for no one really knew for sure. Didn't father worry sometimes, surely he must. It was only human to wonder and speculate a little on whether the coroner's verdict had been absolutely right.

Charles is sensible and matter-of-fact. He says (quite rightly) that I brood too much, look back on things that are over and done with. Never look back, is one of his axioms . . . forward, ever forward, but never, never back. But I'm less strong-minded than he, and I knew it was mainly to be doubly reassured that I was going down to Fawding today. I'd take the 'bus to Fawding and walk around the town. I might even, with a supreme great effort, take a quick look at the Head.

Charles had been surprised when I'd told him I was going to Brighton.

'But darling, nothing's decided yet . . . it's still all in the air.'

'I can go and look round. I can even see if there are any houses up for sale.'

'Don't get involved at this stage.'

'No, I won't but you don't mind me going there, do you Charles?' (I didn't tell him I was going on a pilgrimage to Fawding. He'd have thought I was being morbid again.)

'No, of course not. Have a good day out.' He came over and kissed me and my spirits soared high. Although I vowed I didn't care I knew in my heart I did. Putting our marriage on a better footing was really all I cared *about*, despite the flippant front I put up.

So I sang as I pulled on my wine

corduroy suit, and tied my hair back in a wide chiffon band the colour of peppermint rock. I wouldn't need a coat, the weather had turned warm ... it was a sort of benediction of a day.

So there it is, I thought now rocking in the train. The sea air will do me good, I'll go to Fawding to lay a ghost, and I won't let the thought of what happened to mother haunt me ever again.

I was just wondering whether I'd sway along to the buffet, when the dividing door slid open with a click.

'Is this anyone's seat?' A brown-faced man with bright yellow hair was looking down at me, head bent. He was enormous ... taller even than Charles and broader on the shoulder ... a great blond giant of a man.

'No.' I said stiltedly, looking a little pointedly at the half-dozen other vacant seats. I reached for my magazine and opened it held high. I'm not over-fond of talking to people on trains. I like to sit and think, or simply read in peace, or watch the outside world go flashing by.

The blond man dropped into the opposite seat, slewing slightly sideways to accommodate his length, crossing his legs at the knees. I observed him covertly over the top of my paper: grey socks, a good suit in dark grey, pale lilac shirt and purple tie . . . around twenty-eight or nine, definitely younger than Charles. He was fair but not chilly fair, his blondness held a warmth. I couldn't see the colour of his eyes. He had short thick eyelashes, the colour of sable brushes. He was reading *The Angling Times*.

Then as we shot out of the tunnel and sat blinking in the sun I remembered I'd seen him earlier, going down to the buffet, in the company of an elderly woman in green. He smiled as our eyes met and colour flooded my face. I hoped he hadn't seen me staring hard.

'I may be wrong, please forgive me if

I am, but I think you're Nina . . . Dr. Cullimore's daughter, who used to live at Lemston near King's Lynn.'

'My name was Cullimore . . . I'm Mrs. Redman now.' (Nina, indeed! What a cheek he had!)

'I knew you were married, but I couldn't remember your surname.' He was smiling as if I amused him, and I felt rather cross.

'I don't remember you at all,' I said stiltedly, 'perhaps it was at a party, or something like that?'

'A sort of party, yes . . . a wedding reception, in fact!'

'Whose wedding?'

'My mother's and your father's. I'm Duncan . . . Duncan Stevens . . . we're step-brother and -sister.'

I stared at him speechlessly, my thoughts swinging back . . . laughter, chatter, a thick carpet, the smell of champagne and fruit cake, smoked salmon and cigars. Charles and I chinking our glasses together, drinking a silent toast of our own. We'd been married two weeks then, two short weeks; we'd only just got back from Corfu. No I didn't remember Duncan, I couldn't recall him at all, but then that wasn't surprising really, for my eyes and ears, every fibre of my being had been concentrated solely on Charles.

'I don't remember you,' I answered now, a little more politely, 'but there were so many people there that day.'

'And you were so very newly married!'

'Yes I was!' We laughed together then and shook hands formally, and I thought how nice he was. His blue eyes twinkled, disappeared when he laughed, and a wide friendly smile took possession of his face, shortening the long 'fiddle' chin. He was attractive, very pleasant, and I couldn't help liking him; he had an unusual appeal. I wondered if he were married and what his wife was like. Of course I remembered father mentioning a step-son, but I knew he didn't live at home.

'Duncan, my boy, so you've introduced yourself. Didn't I tell you it was she?'

A knitted coat brushed my knees, a handbag bumped my cheek, and there was the elderly woman in the strange green outfit and the white hair that stuck out in points. She peered at me boldly out of brilliant blue eyes, periwinkle blue eyes like his. Perhaps she was a relative, possibly his grandmother. Her skin was like parchment, criss-crossed with lines.

'Meet my great-aunt, Leila Stevens,' Duncan said briefly, 'Now sit down do, Leila, you're holding up the traffic.' He rose to manoeuvre her into the other half of the seat, and it was then that my memory clicked home. It was seeing them sitting there side by side that brought the past back to mind. Leila had been at the wedding too. I remembered her wielding a camera, taking photographs of us all.

'Duncan's been to fetch me,' she informed me now, 'I have a week with him in the spring and a fortnight in the autumn. He's very pleased to have me. He's not married, you see, so I can please myself what I do once I get there.'

'Oh how nice.'

'He's an antique furniture renovator, with a flat over his workshop near The Lanes. He paints a bit too . . . he's very artistic.'

'Oh, how interesting.' I was beginning to sound like Basil Brush; I probably looked like him too.

'I like Brighton . . . plenty of life.'

'I suppose there is,' I said, feeling rather nonplussed, whilst Duncan caught my eye and smiled.

'Oh come now, darling, that's enough about us. Nina doesn't want to hear all that.'

'I don't remember you at Lemston,' I said, 'when I was living with father, I mean.'

'I rather imagine I'd be at University then. Afterwards I was in business with a friend in Windsor; after that I came down here. My family has always lived in Lemston, though. My father was a G.P. there.'

'Yes, I knew that your mother . . . that Mrs. Stevens was a doctor's widow. I suppose that's why . . . ' I broke off in confusion, as I realised what I'd said, my discomfiture not lessened by Leila's piercing stare which had the effect of nailing me to my seat.

'And didn't your dear mother meet with some kind of accident?' she asked, obviously looking forward to my reply.

'She went over the cliff edge at Fawding Head.'

'*Fell* over?'

'Yes.'

Her breath hissed inwards, her blue eyes gleamed.

'But of course, how dreadful! I remember Valerie telling me . . . a verdict of accidental death.'

I nodded, unable to speak. I was swallowing hard.

'But how lovely that Valerie and your father married dear . . . such a suitable match . . . she's such a help to him. And after all, life goes on, one can't live with the dead.'

'Where are you living these days, Nina?' I was thankful to excruciation point when Duncan intervened. With relief I took my eyes off the face of his great-aunt, and looked with more pleasure on his.

'At Cranston Heath, not far from Croydon. Charles, my husband, works in Town.'

'At the Foreign Office?' enquired Leila, once more agog.

'Not the Foreign Office.'

'Intelligence then . . . Fraud Squad . . . Special Branch C.I.D.?'

'He's a solicitor,' I replied shortly, hoping to damp her down, and I smiled as I met Duncan's gaze. His eyes were like Leila's, yet there was a world of difference. His dwelt gently, hers pierced through, his narrowed in laughter, hers slit in zeal. She made me feel like a raw scraped potato, he took the trouble to be kind. His face was kind too, not jutting, not tough. It was masculine, yet dreamy, as though he dwelt inside his head, as though he thought about things a lot. He was what I would describe as a bookish type of man. My father had been like that.

'Where exactly do you live in Brighton?' I searched around for something to say.

'In a maisonette over my workshop in Bazely Street. It used to be an office at one time. There's plenty of space which is what I like. And I need storage room if I get a lot of work.'

'Are you going to Brighton for the day, Miss Cullimore?' This was Leila determined to intrude.

'My name's Nina Redman, and yes I am going to Brighton. My husband and I may be coming this way to live. I thought I'd have a look round at house property and . . . and things.'

'Any children?'

'No.'

'Pity. Marriage needs children, they make another link. Still . . . ' she scratched a bony knee, displaying black mesh tights, then wrapped her coat around them again, 'plenty of time for you, you're no age yet. People have babies knocking fifty these days, easy as popping a pod. Duncan,' she turned to him abruptly, digging her elbow into his side, 'didn't you say you knew of a house — the one you thought you might buy and then decided against, the one that belongs to your friend Mr. Lee, the one that's full of antiques?'

Duncan looked embarrassed and shifted in his seat, 'Leila you're going too fast. I really don't think . . . '

'Show her over it this afternoon. Ask her to have lunch with us. Afterwards we could all go over . . . '

'Thank you, but no!' The words shot out of me more quickly than I'd intended, but the old lady was a menace, making all these plans, arranging my lunch and afternoon with great enthusiasm, without so much as a single enquiry as to whether I might be free. This day was mine to do what I liked with. I didn't want to spend it with either of the Stevens. 'I already have an appointment for lunch,' I continued, 'and my afternoon is spoken for, every single minute.'

'Oh but I thought you said . . . '

'Leave it, Leila, you're embarrassing Nina. I expect she prefers to do her househunting through an agent. It's hardly up to us to interfere.'

The old lady bristled, but lapsed into silence, and I threw Duncan a grateful glance. He was evidently well able to nip her in the bud, which considering she was spending her holiday with him was probably a very good thing. He must be a very kind man to take her on at all; she'd have sent me round the bend in an hour.

The train halted briefly at Preston Park, then rocked and joggled slowly into Brighton itself. The atmosphere in our part of the carriage wasn't good, and I was sorry to realise that my fit of rebellion had completely dried the conversation up. I hadn't meant that.

43

I'd wanted to talk to Duncan, but his great-aunt had spoilt things with her continual butting in. I was glad when we all left the train.

I said goodbye to them in the station forecourt, and seizing the opportunity whilst Leila bought a paper, I told Duncan I was sorry I'd slightly blown my top. He looked down at me gravely from his great blond height.

'It's I who should apologise. I know what Leila's like. When she starts making plans she's as difficult to push back as the sea was to old King Canute. I thought you dealt with her very well indeed, and you were politeness itself, I might add.'

'Thank goodness for that, because I'm very often rude, and I know I tend to get uptight. Charles is always telling me about it; he's very cool himself, although there are occasions when he blows up too.'

'Well, when you get down here, when you're living here, you'll have to get Charles interested in broken down antiques, and make my business boom even more than it does already.'

'Does it boom?'

'No, worse luck! But it keeps me in reasonable style, and I'm doing the type of work I enjoy.'

'That must be very rewarding,' I breathed, just as Leila reappeared, brandishing the *Argus*, the wind playing havoc with her hair.

'Has she changed her mind?' she whispered sibilantly to Duncan, and he laughed and turned her round to the kerb.

'No, she hasn't. She's dying to get rid of us, but she's hiding it adroitly, she's a very courteous girl. Well, goodbye, Nina . . . good to have met you again. Good hunting too, and the very best of luck!'

'Thank you very much . . . goodbye!' I raised my hand in a wave, watching the tall rangy man and the short spiky woman make their way over to the taxis on the rank.

I walked into Queen's Road and down into the town, a little undecided what to do. I'd been going to treat myself to a rather splendid lunch, but in the end I settled for a sandwich in a bar and caught a tall green 'bus which had Eastbourne on the front and which I knew called at Fawding as well. I'd make my pilgrimage first, *then* come back to Brighton. I'd get the worst over first and then forget about it.

★ ★ ★

Fawding hadn't changed much. I saw that as soon as I got out in the High Street and smelled the salty tang of the sea. It was the smell that did it, it took me instantly back. It wasn't so much nostalgia as a retraction into my girlhood, to a time when my life had been bounded by school and home, when all important decisions had been taken off my hands, when responsibility was a thing unknown.

I was seventeen again with my hair chunked off in points, mainly because a youth had told me I had a smile like

Audrey Hepburn and I'd just seen the TV version of *Roman Holiday*. I was a girl again, buying make-up in Boots, having tea with mother in the continental *patisserie*, going to rave-ups in the hall at the end of the pier.

I sighed. So much had happened since then . . . so much, *too* much and far too quickly. If only one could go back and do it all over again, in a different way, in an adult way, acting sensibly, not impulsively, not dashing at things.

I walked the length of the High Street to the fork at the end, where one prong continued as shops and offices and the other tailed off into houses and hotels as one got nearer and nearer to the front. I walked until I reached the doctor's house, which had once been my home; I went and stood by the gate. It brought back another kaleidoscope of memories and I leaned against the rough wall, drinking it all in. Grey stone, double-fronted, with dull green shutters . . . not a beautiful house, but solid, standing four-square to the wind. The garden was flourishing too, despite its proximity to the sea. It was full of red tulips, the pointed parrot kind. A bed of tawny wallflowers perfumed the westerly breeze. A breeze was all right, it did no real harm, but an on-shore gale could turn a beautiful garden into a salt-encrusted wilderness overnight. Mother had struggled with the garden, pitting her skills against the elements. 'I'll never, never, never give up,' she'd said. Mother had been a person who could never resist a challenge . . . throw down the gauntlet and she'd have to pick it up. I suppose that was the way she'd been made.

I lingered by the gate, a new gate, an oak one. We'd had an old painted one before. I wanted to go in, but of course I knew I couldn't. There was a perambulator in the porch, a space-hopper on the lawn. Father's successor had been a young man who was obviously, now, a family one. He'd probably got two or three children, maybe even four. Seven years was a long time ago.

The Head hadn't changed either. It looked just the same . . . a steep rise of cliff, like a hunched green shoulder thrusting up high in the sky. But to get the full impact one had to stand on the shore, to stand at its base and look neck-breakingly up at that great white bastion of chalk. It is said that in Roman times Caesar's men camped on the Head, and from round about, on the surounding hills other armies had lain in watch for three different armadas — Hitler's, Napoleon's and the King of Spain's. It seemed that there had always been armies in Fawding; Canadian soldiers had been billeted there during the war in readiness for the raid on Dieppe.

So the Head couldn't change. It was pretty well unchangeable. It was time-less, ageless, merciless too. I shuddered and turned away.

It was more rough here. The weather seemed to have worsened in keeping with my mood. The wind tore at my hair, blew coldly through my skirt. I began the walk down the ramp to the front, my eyes turned away from the cliff. Did father ever think about my mother these days? Did he wake in the night, as I often did, and ever think, ever wonder what really happened, up on the Head that day? He had tried to comfort me, he had done his level best. 'She must have died instantly,' he'd told me gently, 'even before her body struck the rocks.' She'd been found by a schoolmaster and a party of boys who were studying the shore at low tide.

I reached the promenade and leaned against the rail. This visit was silly. I shouldn't have come. But what would it be like when I was living here again? Of course, Brighton was different . . . not remote like this. It wasn't remote, nor slightly desolate as it was out here; even the gulls didn't sound so mournful in Brighton . . . it was much more cheerful all round.

The sea heaved and rocked, reared

into foam, rattled back noisily on the steeply shelving beach. Out on the horizon, just visible in the fret, I could see a trail of thick black smoke:

'Dirty British coaster with a salt-
    caked smoke-stack
Chugging through the Channel on
    a mad March day . . . '

School and homework and mother again . . . testing me out for the end of term exams. We'd had such fun together, she and I. Father was the serious one, mother had been gay. I was supposed to be like her, but I didn't feel I was. Most of the time I was painfully sure I'd never be care-free again.

'So this is the way you househunt, is it?'

Startled I turned to see Duncan Stevens at the kerb. Behind him was an estate car with something lodged in the back. There was no sign of Leila this time.

'F . . . fancy seeing you!' I felt foolish

and conscious of my wind-tangled hair, of the streaked wet mess of my face. If he noticed he gave no sign, merely stood at my side.

'I've been collecting a bookcase from The Grange,' he said, 'I've an antique dealer friend whose van has broken down. If you've finished I could give you a lift into Brighton, I'm on my way back there now.'

'It's very good of you.' I hesitated, biting my lip.

'Nina, haven't you been dragging about long enough on your own? You look just about all in.'

'I've been visiting old haunts.'

'Sentimental journeys can be very exhausting, particularly when the weather's well and truly on the downgrade. It's going to pour with rain.' A smile bent his mouth, but his eyes were concerned. It was nice of him to mind . . . good of him to help. Perhaps I'd go with him, get an early train, be at home when Charles got in.

'I'd like a lift very much,' I said,

making up my mind.

'Good.' He helped me into the car, went round to his side and folded himself behind the steering wheel. His shoulder brushed mine as he bent to release the brake, his face was a few inches from mine. I was acutely aware of the force of his attraction . . . the first dart of warning shot home.

Being married is misleading. When you enter that state you are perfectly certain that never, never, ever, will any other male attract you ever again. But of course they do . . . human nature sees to that. You just have to be civilised and sensible and loyal, and concentrate hard all the time.

I concentrated on the bookcase which nudged me in the neck as the car swung away from the kerb.

'That thing bothering you? I did my best to wedge it. Normally I don't do this kind of boy scout act, but I made an exception this time.'

'It's not bothering me at all. I'm . . . I'm glad to have a lift.'

'Going straight back home?'

'Yes.'

'Have tea with me in Brighton before you get your train. It's early yet and I'd like to talk to you. We could go to the Old Ship, do it in style.'

'I'd rather . . . I mean I'd better get home.'

'Fair enough . . . just as you like.'

We didn't talk a lot on the rest of the journey. The traffic was heavy on the main coast road, and it was raining in earnest, making driving difficult, slapping against the windscreen and bucketing on the roof. I stretched my legs and leaned back. It was a warm and very comfortable car, in spite of the bookcase which made its presence felt every time Duncan changed gear. We were dropping down into Rottingdean now. The White Horse Hotel, St. Dunstan's, Roedean School, Black Rock, then Kemp Town and the Palace Pier, we were very nearly there.

'So it's straight to the station then? You won't change your mind?'

'No, I'd better not,' she said, 'but thank you all the same.'

'What were you visiting in the way of old haunts?' he asked me as we waited at the barrier for my train which had so far not come in.

'My old home and Fawding Head.'

'Fawding Head? You didn't go climbing up there in this wind?'

'No, I just looked.'

'With your mother in mind, of course.'

I nodded, at a loss, emotion gripping me again.

'Nina . . . ' his arm came round my shoulders to draw me on one side as a porter with a trolley pushed by, 'Nina, at the risk of sounding callous, it's a long time ago . . . shouldn't you have . . . '

'Put it behind me . . . forgotten about it?' I looked up at him feeling just slightly outraged. It was all right for him, his mother was alive, and doing jolly well for herself with father to hold her hand. 'Yes I know I ought to have accepted it now, Charles is always telling me so, but what one should and shouldn't do, and actually has to and does do, are often two different things. I mean to be sensible, I don't think about it often, but it's there nevertheless and coming down here's made it worse. If only I knew *exactly* what happened . . . I really could let go then.'

'Your mother must have wanted to look over the edge . . . the edge has a queer sort of fascination somehow . . . '

'And then she turned dizzy?'

'Well yes, she may have done . . . she *must* have done Nina, and you'll really have to square up to it, you know, particularly if you're coming down this way to live.'

'I almost hope we don't now.'

'But if your husband's job brings him . . . '

'He can please himself, he's a partner, he can do as he likes. Anyway a move won't solve anything much.' I think I'd forgotten I was speaking aloud, forgotten whom I was with.

'Solve anything?' Duncan's eyebrows rose . . . 'Is there a problem then?'

'Oh no . . . no of course not!' Fortunately I think he thought I was still talking about mother, for he went on to say, holding my hand in his.

'There's only one proper way of laying your ghost, and that is to take it by the scruff of its neck and give it a jolly good shake!'

'Do ghosts have scruffs?' The conversation had lightened and I laughed in return. All I wanted to do was get home.

'I'm sure they do, so the next time you're down here give me a ring and we'll trek up together to the top of the Head and stand there and drink in the view.'

'I have been there.'

'But not since.'

'No, not . . . since.'

'Well then, that's a date.' His voice was jocular, but his eyes were grave. It occurred to me then that he was the sort of man who'd never let anyone down.

'Duncan . . . '

'Yes?'

'Oh nothing . . . it's all right, I'd better go through.' The train had come in and was rhythmically thrumming which meant it wanted to start. I passed through the barrier, dropping his hand, 'Thank you for the lift . . . it was a very great help.'

'Any time, only too willing. And think over what I said.'

'I will, I promise.'

'Goodbye, Nina.'

'Goodbye, Duncan.'

I walked up the platform alongside the train, turning just once to wave yet again at the tall fair man in the dark grey suit standing underneath the station clock.

★   ★   ★

In spite of the fact that I'd caught an early train, Charles was home before me that night. I could hear the hiss of the shower as I ran up the stairs, hear him clear his throat in the particular way he had, hum the Eton Boating Song as he dried his back.

He came into the bedroom whilst I was peeling off my suit, wearing his towelling bathrobe and vigorously drying his hair. He looked pleased to see me; he also looked carefree, as though some kind of happening had eased his mind.

'You're home early, poppet. Enjoy yourself?'

'Oh . . . so, so. But it was cold, the weather changed after lunch.'

'Didn't entirely come up to expectations then?'

'What a ham expression!'

'Well . . . did it?' He stood close behind me as I sat in front of the dressing table. He bent and kissed the top of my head.

'No it didn't . . . not really.'

'So it wouldn't break your heart if we *didn't* live there?'

'What do you mean?' Weren't we going then . . . weren't we going . . . what was he going to say?

His lips brushed my ear, I smelt soap on his skin, his chin was just the slightest bit rough. There's something about the beard of a man that . . . 'Negotiations for the lease of the Brighton office premises have well and truly broken down.'

The back of my hairbrush bumped against my forehead. I let it fall into my lap.

'You mean we won't be going . . . we're *never* going?' Was I pleased . . . did I mind . . . what did I feel?

'Never's a long time my darling, but not in the foreseeable future I'm afraid. Do you mind so very much . . . do you really mind?'

Our eyes met in the mirror . . . his questioning, faintly worried, mine trying to hide what I felt. Uppermost was relief, but I wouldn't let him see it. He shouldn't have raised my hopes and then dashed them down, even with the cautionary note attached. Supposing I'd come back from Brighton all crazy to move there . . . it was all very well to say sorry at this stage . . . he shouldn't have mentioned the chance of it at the start. You're being unfair Nina Redman, and well you know it. For goodness sake let him off the hook.

'Nina . . . ' His voice in my ear had a loud throbbing quality. I leaned forward, away from him, tying back my hair.

'Well it looks as though we're back to square one again.'

'Is that so bad?'

I couldn't bear the anxious look in his eyes. I smiled at him in the mirror, I capitulated at once, I could never be proof against Charles.

He pulled me to my feet, turned me round to face him, held me tight-loosely so that I curved in his arms. 'Nina my darling . . . my darling Nina!'

As I felt him lift me my last clear thought was of a tall cliff topped with bright green sward, of the breeze in the grass, of the cry of a gull, and the soft insistent murmur of the sea.

3

About three weeks later I was in the kitchen trying out a new kind of quiche, when the telephone rang and it was Charles' Uncle Jocelyn, inviting me out to lunch.

'Janina? Is that you my dear?' I recognised the hollow honking voice the second I heard it, and waited with bated breath for the invitation I knew would come and which Charles wouldn't like one bit.

'Yes it's me, Uncle Joce, how nice to hear you.' I wiped oniony hands on the front of my jeans and sat down on the hall chair.

'Isn't it time you came up to Town again, young lady. I haven't set eyes on you since Crufts.'

'No, we . . . I haven't been up for ages actually.'

'Well that, if I may say so, must be

remedied at once. Come and have lunch with me next Thursday at the Club. I'll meet you in the cocktail bar just before one.'

I hesitated, stalled, but only for a second. It wouldn't do not to seem keen. An invitation from Uncle Joce was akin to a Royal command; in any case I knew I'd enjoy a trip to Town, and to lunch de luxe in the pomp of Pall Mall was a chance one didn't get every day. So of course I thanked him, and we chatted some more, and he eventually honk-honked off.

The quiche out of the oven, I made myself some coffee and took it into the loggia with my gardening paper. I closed the blinds slightly against the glare of the sun. It was greenhouse hot as the loggia faced south and soaked up the sun like a sponge. Not that I minded, I adored being warm, the sun made me kind of expand.

It was May now, the flowering month, and the garden was looking its best with the lilacs and laburnums and cherry trees all out, scattering the lawn with bloom. In some ways I think May's my favourite time of year, the air is soft and full of scents and there's a promise, a magic, a bursting into life, the whole of nature geared to sliding straight into summer.

But 'the grass is always greener . . . ' as everyone knows, and I couldn't help thinking how lovely it would be in Sussex, all blue and golden and those softly sloping Downs. Still, I stretched luxuriously and lay back in my chair, it was lovely here too in its way. Charles and I had been getting on rather better lately. I was more content and he was less edgy, and although we were wary, treading delicately like Agag, we did seem to be moving off the shifting sand, and we certainly argued less. So in some ways it was unfortunate that Uncle Joce had rung, because Charles didn't like me seeing him much.

Uncle Jocelyn is Sir William's brother, but is twenty years his junior, which makes him knocking sixty, I suppose.

He's of medium height and square with faded red hair; he has blue eyes that 'pop' and a bull-doggish chin. He invariably looks pink as though he's hot inside and he's always full to bursting with ideas. He's a tycoon in his way, being on the boards of several companies and chairman of the famous Crosfield Tea Group which takes him abroad a good deal. In nature he's the overriding, dominant type, which is why Charles avoids him when he can.

'He's so self-opinionated, Nina. He explodes his ideas and theories like sticks of gelignite. He doesn't care a fig whom he destroys in the process . . . he has to have everything his way!'

'He puts a lot of business in your firm's way.'

'We can do without him.'

That was the way the conversation always went when we got on to the subject of Uncle Joce. So I knew Charles wouldn't be pleased about my luncheon date, and I only hoped it wouldn't provoke a scene. His reaction that evening, when I told him the news, was very much as I feared it would be.

'Oh, darling, really . . . couldn't you have put him off?'

'I couldn't think of anything on the spur of the moment.'

'I thought he'd given up trying to manage us. Now you're not to tell him anything about what goes on. Don't give him the faintest hint of anything at all.'

'About what, for heaven's sake? There's nothing to give away, no cat to let out of the bag, no grooey skeleton in the cupboard under the stairs!'

'I'm not joking, Nina!'

I saw to my amazement and considerable dismay that the old tense expression was back on Charles' face. He hadn't even laughed at my feeble little joke.

'Don't worry, Charles. It'll be all right. Actually I never do say much to Uncle Joce. For one thing it's impossible to get a word in, and for another there simply isn't time. He gives me a cocktail, then lunch, then coffee, then dashes back to his board meeting or desk. He doesn't spend the afternoon airing me in the park, or buying me lush jewellery in the shops.'

'His imagination works overtime too, so don't worry about anything he says.'

'I never do, it flows over me like lava fresh from the pot. When you come to think about it he's a bit like a volcano, erupting with a great big whoof and spuffle, blowing out clouds of smoke.'

I was still trying hard to make Charles smile, to take the rigid look off his face. But he grunted and opened the paper and I could tell he was cross by the way he kept bashing it and snatching at the leaves. All the same I was taken aback when a full hour later he put down his knife and fork and said.

'Couldn't you put him off?'

'What?'

'Uncle Joce . . . couldn't you put him off?'

'But, Charles, no, of course not!' I

choked on a potato and stared at him in concern. Whatever was the matter with him, whatever did he mean? He'd never been as anti-Uncle-Joce as this before. He usually came round in the end. 'I can't not go, Charles. I've said that I will. I can't put him off, it'd be so rude.'

'You could say you're not feeling well . . . ring him up the day before.'

This was so unlike Charles who's a stickler for the truth that I could hardly believe my own ears. 'I can't do that . . . he'd see right through it — either that or come beetling down here. You know what he is; he wouldn't take it lying down.'

'You could think of something, or we could between us. Nina, I really mean it . . . I'm asking you not to go.'

'But why . . . *why*? You've got to tell me *why*! Is there something the matter, something you've not told me?' The old uncertainties came rushing back, my hand shook so violently I had to put down my glass. The tension in the air was almost electric . . . I felt poised on the edge of it all.

'Oh for God's sake!' He flung down his napkin and got up from the table. 'For God's sake don't get on to that tack again. I'm simply asking you, as your husband, please *not to go*!' His eyes met mine angrily as he leaned over my chair. He looked as though he hated me and I went quite cold inside.

'But you're not asking me, are you . . . ' my voice came out shakily, then steadied in fury, 'you're not asking me, you're telling me, you're ordering me to stay. You're giving me orders, you're *telling* me what to do . . . you're as domineering as he is . . . you'll be like him one day. But this time I'm not going to do as you say. I'm not going to be rude and unkind to an old man just because you say so, Charles!'

'So you're defying me!'

'If you like to put it that way . . . yes!' I was on my feet now and we stood there tensed like tigers. Hate was jarring through me now . . . I could be as hurtful as he. 'You should have married a doormat Charles . . . a dear little fluffy one, like a little lamb . . . a little sheep-like girl who'd agree with you all the while . . . yes, Charles . . . no, Charles . . . three bags full, Charles . . . every time you opened your mouth!'

'You should have had the word 'obey' scored from the marriage service!'

'There should never have been a marriage service!'

There was a moment of silence . . . a silence so complete, it seemed to strike an actual blow.

'What did you say?'

'There should never have been a marriage service . . . we should never have got married! I don't like being ordered about, I hate being tied, I hate not having a useful job, I hate being treated as though I'm nothing and nobody. It's all a let-down . . . I don't like it . . . I . . . '

'Janina!' The look on his face should have warned me to stop, but I was too pent-up to care.

'I'm sorry but it's true . . . it's true . . . it's true! I wish I still worked for father, I wish my mother were alive, I wish we'd never married. I wish we were free to walk away from each other . . . we've exhausted every ounce of what there was between us, and I don't want to go on any more!'

I felt my stomach lurch. I pushed past him and fled. I tore into the bathroom, bolting myself in. Retching into the lavatory I crouched on the floor, I leaned back limply against the wall.

The floor heaved, the walls sagged, pink and black tiles made a crazy mosaic, bath and basin merged into one. I closed my eyes, I clung to the bath. Soon it would pass . . . soon I could think . . . soon I could decide what I must do after the terrible things I had said.

But thinking made it worse, I was appalled at myself. I couldn't have said it . . . I couldn't have said it . . . I couldn't have said that to Charles. Yet I had, and what was worse it scraped very near the truth. Now that it was out it couldn't be put back in . . . it was like Pandora's Box.

All the same I'd got to try, I'd got to put back the lid. I didn't, *couldn't* hurt him, and we'd got to live together. It was up to me to try and make things right.

I washed my face, ran a comb through my hair, drank a glass of water from the bathroom tap, and went slowly and deliberately downstairs. I felt sick again as I crossed the hall, put my hand on the knob of the sitting room door, twisted it and walked inside. Please, Charles, be nice to me . . . please let me make amends.

He was sitting in his chair, his face very white. He wasn't reading, nor working, just staring at the door. He jumped to his feet as I crossed to his side. I felt it might be all right.

'I lost my temper, Charles, I didn't really mean it.'

'I provoked you, I was unreasonable.

I'm sorry too.' He kissed me, we clung a little, the episode was closed.

But the quarrel lay between us like a sword.

★ ★ ★

During the next few days I wore my flippant face. Neither of us mentioned the impending luncheon date. Charles must have known that I still meant to go, but I didn't like to bring it up myself. I was therefore relieved when on Thursday at breakfast, he spoke about it naturally as though he didn't mind a bit.

'How about coming round to the office when you've finished with Uncle Joce. I'll get off early, we could do something in Town . . . go and see Tutankhamun if you can wait in the queue.'

I'd been wanting to see the exhibition ever since it opened. 'It'd be super,' I said shakily, hardly daring to breathe, 'I'll come round for you just before four.'

I felt very trembly as he kissed me goodbye. I also felt guilty and strained. He was trying to put things right, but the quarrel had been my fault. I'd been obstinate and nasty, sticking up for my rights. Perhaps women shouldn't have rights once they were married, or at least not specific ones, not ones they should insist on. It was necessary to blend in marriage, to kind of jell together. The old cocoon of singleness had to be thrown away.

I wondered if other people found marriage difficult. How, for instance did Tim and Dallas get on? There was one thing quite certain, Dallas didn't blend with Tim ... she was married yet seemed free as air too. She and Tim hardly ever seemed to be together, but they appeared to be happy, there was no talk of divorce. I had the utmost admiration for Dal. She was Hungari-anborn, but brought up in Canada as her parents had emigrated there. She never, so Charles told me, took to British ways, and after she and Tim had been married about a year, she left him on his own and went back to Toronto, living with her parents again. She was away for months and months, and just as the conventional Redmans were wondering what the score was, back she came, happy as Larry, ready to start off again. And from then on that had been the pattern of their marriage ... six months on, six months off — the best of both worlds for Dal.

I thought it was a funny arrangement, but if I ever expressed surprise to Charles, he'd shrug his shoulders and say. 'Live and let live ... we're all different, you know ... we all have our own ways of making things work.' He was uncharacteristically airy about it, which puzzled me a great deal.

Still, right at this minute Tim and Dal were together, living in their service flat in Sloane Street, Knightsbridge. Tim was an accountant and worked in Mark Lane. I think Charles met him at lunchtimes occasionally, but he's never really told me much about his brother, and neither Tim nor Dal had been to 'High Walls' more than six times in two years.

★ ★ ★

It was nearly one o'clock when I reached Uncle Joce's Club and heaved my way round the heavy revolving doors. I went straight into the cocktail bar, escorted by a page, and there was Uncle Joce, all peppery and hot, strumming with his fingers on the arm of his chair, glaring towards the doors. He got to his feet the second he saw me and crossing the sea of carpet at a very brisk trot, enveloped me in a bear-like embrace.

'Janina, my dear, marvellous to see you! You're looking absolutely superb!'

I was wearing a mustard dress in Chinese silk, long-sleeved, banded at the wrists. I'd brushed my hair down flat, tying it tightly in the nape, so that it hung down long at the back. This was the way that Charles liked it best and it suited the style of my dress.

Uncle Joce's hand was cupping my elbow, guiding me to a chair, where he ordered a Campari for us both.

'You and Charles all right?'

'Yes, fine, thank you.' I met his eye full on, over the rim of my glass, and hastily looked away.

'He's a lucky fellow . . . by Jove he's a lucky chap!'

'Thank you.' It was pleasant to be complimented, even by Uncle Joce who, despite his age, was very much a 'ladies' man'.

Throughout lunch, which was perfection, washed down with Nuits St. Georges, Uncle Joce made his usual enquiries about us all; but it wasn't until we were in the coffee lounge that he really got down to the business of the day, and so to speak spread himself out.

I'd suspected all through lunch that he'd something special to impart, but his eyes had shone and bolted even more than usual and he'd had a very high colour indeed. Now in the lounge he was even more uptight, cracking his knuckles and slapping his knees and dragging at the lobes of his ears. I poured out his coffee and he gulped it down in one, his nose sticking out over the absurd little cup, his thick sandy eyebrows furred. There was a ring on his little finger that blindingly caught the light; it was probably a diamond ... a diamond solitaire; there was another on his tie in the centre of a pin, he would call them investments, of course.

'Janina ... young Tim's leaving Latimers!'

I put down my cup, marshalling all my concentration, not an easy task on an alcoholised stomach, which was fast affecting my head.

'Left Latimers?'

'His firm girl ... his firm!'

'You mean he was sacked, made redundant?'

A strong whiff of aniseed came wafting over the table ... Kimmel being Uncle's pet liqueur. 'Good Lord no . . . redundant, not likely . . . he's left them of his own accord.'

'But why?'

'Because I told him to, urged him to do so; more or less insisted that he did.'

'But why?' I asked again, still not very interested, but feeling I should show some concern.

'Because it's the best possible thing for the boy, all things considered. I've been on to him about it for months.'

'He has got a new job then?'

'I got it for him.'

'Oh I see,' I said lamely, lapsing into silence. Perhaps the best thing was not to comment, but to let Uncle Joce explain, tell me in his own explosive way. And he did just that. He was bursting with it. It must have been gnawing at him all through lunch, all through the duck and orange sauce. And of course it was his reason for asking me here today. But why me and not Charles, heaven only knew. There was no space to ask even one question now, so I sipped my creme-de-menthe and coffee in alternate dribs and drabs, and settled myself down in my chair. For a long time the main sound in that cool elegant room was the unmelodious sea-lion honk of Uncle Jocelyn's voice.

Personally I thought he was boosting Tim too high. Charles could have done just as well. And it was ordinary enough news, goodness knows. A vacancy had arisen in one of Uncle Joce's companies. It was the post of Company Secretary to Andersons Foods, a big group concern with supermarkets and stores in England and overseas as well. Uncle Joce had merely seen to it that Tim was on the short-list.

'And after that it was plain sailing, Janina. There were no other applicants to touch Tim. Of course if he hadn't been a chartered accountant and served some years in a 'stable' like Latimers, I couldn't have backed him for one single minute. As things were it was a certainty, the Board snapped him up.

And it's a good thing, you know . . . it's time he struck out. Tim has to be pushed, otherwise he doesn't bother . . . he's content to stagnate like a lily in a pond . . . can't see what's under his nose.'

'I like Tim.'

'Oh he's likeable enough, but no backbone, no guts, never puts up a good fight. This'll be the making of him, be better all round.'

'Is he pleased about it?'

'*Pleased!*' Uncle Joce reddened as though I'd insulted him . . . 'Pleased . . . course he's pleased . . . he's absolutely delighted . . . can't thank me enough. It's exactly what he needs and he's got the sense to see it!'

'I expect you're right.'

'Right . . . of course I'm right . . . I know about these things!' He drank another cup of coffee, his Adam's apple bobbed. 'They'll be living in Canada you know. Head Office is in Toronto. They'll be leaving in three weeks' time.'

I straightened in my chair, I *was*

interested now. 'In Canada, but that's Dal's home, her parents live there! She'll be absolutely thrilled Uncle Joce . . . it's exactly what she wants!'

'It'll settle their marital differences . . . keep them together. You can't make a marriage work living half your time apart. A man and his wife should cleave together; that's the essence of the contract as it were.'

'But Uncle Joce . . . '

'Now look, my dear . . . ' a large hot hand alighted on my knee, then just as suddenly moved off again. 'If Dallas hankers after a life in Canada then Tim's got to follow suit.'

'Shouldn't it be the other way round? And if Dallas and Tim are seriously incompatible then I can't see that Canada or Timbuctoo are going to make them change.'

Uncle Joce looked peeved, very slightly dashed. Perhaps he'd thought of this too, but had ruthlessly dismissed it under the wheels of 'getting young Tim on his way'. 'Well we shall see, won't we

. . . we shall see. I don't like to see young couples drifting apart. It's messy, untidy, leads to all sorts of trouble.'

'But . . .'

'Janina, there are things I'm aware of, of which you have no knowledge. Allow me to be the best judge.'

'Does Charles know Tim's going off to Canada?'

'Tim's going to ring him today . . . they'll probably be lunching together. I told Tim to keep quiet about it up until today.'

'Charles will be very surprised,' I said quietly, 'he thought Tim was at Latimers for good. He won't like not being kept in the picture. And Tim *is* his brother . . . surely that counts for something.'

'Pshaw! Rot! Sentimental bull! They've never been close . . . they weren't as boys . . . fought over every mortal thing. In the end it was always your Charles who won . . . except in one instance, of course.'

I was just going to ask him what that

instance was. when I happened to catch sight of the time.

'Uncle, it's half-past three. I'm meeting Charles at four. We're going along to the British Museum to see the Tutankhamun treasures.'

'Are you?' He looked approving. 'Good for you . . . good for you . . . best thing you can do!'

'Husbands and wives do go out together sometimes.'

'Course they do . . . course they do. You're all right, are you . . . you and Charles?'

'What do you mean by all right?' I picked up my shoulder bag, looking at him crossly, now he really *was* trying to probe.

'Everything in the garden's lovely, is it?'

'Down to the last bay leaf.' I assured him, getting to my feet before he pried some more, 'And now I really must be going. Thank you very much for a perfectly lovely lunch.'

'Pleasure my dear.'

We shared a taxi as far as Norfolk Street. Here I got out and Uncle Joce bobbed on, en route for his plateglass office in the heart of Mincing Lane.

4

A week before Tim and Dallas were due to leave for Canada, I suggested that we asked them to 'High Walls' for the day, but Charles didn't seem too keen.

'It'd have to be Sunday and I've got that planned out.'

'But we ought to ask them. It might be ages before you see Tim again, and he *is* your brother . . . surely you mind?'

He made a gesture of irritation and lit his cigarette, 'You make an awful fetish of the cosy family life image. Tim'll be back in this country at least twice a year, and I'm seeing him next week in Town.'

I dug my heels in, refusing to budge. 'But *I'd* like to see him and Dallas too.'

'You hardly know Dal.'

'I like what I know. Oh, Charles, do let's ask them. We could do our jobs on Saturday, leave Sunday free. I could probably get a turkey and cut it up cold, especially if this hot spell keeps on.'

In the end he agreed, but with obvious reluctance. There were times when I didn't understand him at all. He seemed to deliberately make himself obtuse, so that I couldn't see through. Dead on twelve o'clock the following Sunday morning, Tim and Dallas arrived. Tim was just the same, trying to crack feeble jokes and swallowing our best cream sherry as though it were lemonade. Dallas was exactly as I remembered her last . . . ash blonde, blue-eyed, nymph-like in a filmy dress in a pastel smoky shade. She and Tim seemed perfectly all right together. I couldn't sense any antipathy between them. If they were 'on thin ice' as was the belief of Uncle Joce, then they hid it well from anyone looking on.

It was between Tim and Charles that awkwardness showed, revealing itself in an embarrassing forced jollity, the kind people put on at Christmas-time because it's the right thing to do. Occasionally, though, there were nasty barbed remarks that each of them seized on, blew up to life size. The atmosphere was such that it could be cut with a knife . . . they were obviously spoiling for a row.

Good Lord, I thought, why didn't Charles warn me that he was on such bad terms with Tim. I would never have asked them down here if he'd told me the truth . . . why put up a smoke-screen and let me think that the two brothers got along well.

Dal knew, of course. I saw her glance at them once or twice and smile as if to herself. She seemed to me to be rather enjoying it, but not so me, and it was a blessed relief when after lunch Charles suggested we went to see Sir William, so that Tim and Dal could make their farewells.

'Oh, I don't want to come, Charles.' This was Dal, looking bored.

Tim took her up on it, looking red and cross (he has the same kind of colouring as Charles). 'Oh come off it, Dal! You might at least go through the motions. It'll please the old man no end.'

'No, I'm not coming. I'll stay here on my ownsome and have a little nap.' She yawned and stretched like a pale yellow cat, elongating her slim supple body, raising her arms above her head.

I saw Charles look at her, then glance swiftly away. He appeared to be as out of patience as Tim undoubtedly was. It was obviously up to me to save the day.

'Oh look,' I said, stubbing out my cigarette, 'I've got the father and mother of a headache. I don't feel like motoring out to Horley Wood. Dallas and I will stay here in the garden. You two go off together. It'll be nice for father-in-law to have just the two of you, and Dal and I can have a good chat.'

Charles frowned prodigiously and looked upset. Tim grinned and blew me a kiss.

'Well that suits me . . . on your own

head be it, Nina . . . ignorance is bliss and all that!'

'What on earth does he mean?' I asked, as Tim's sports car roared down the drive and Dallas and I collected chairs from the shed. We spread ourselves out on two canvas loungers underneath the elm tree at the back of the house.

'Oh I don't know. Tim's wet at times!' Dal tucked her arms behind her head and her sleeves fell back showing slim pale arms smooth as water lily stems. I looked at her and marvelled. I felt a pang of envy.

'I wish I were blonde,' I said.

'Why for Pete's sake?' Dal turned amused eyes in my direction . . . pale blue-green eyes, the colour of the sea, framed in long curling lashes which she must have had to tint, considering the paleness of her hair. 'You're attractive enough in your way, Nina . . . a black-haired Milanese type with great dark eyes.'

'Black-haired gypsy, more like!' But I

warmed to her slightly, Dal could be charming when she liked.

'Aren't you thrilled to be going to Canada to live? It's marvellous for you, isn't it because it's actually your home . . . your childhood home, I mean?'

She opened her eyes and looked at me sleepily, the sun shining through the branches of the tree making little lacy patterns on her face. 'I can go there when I want anyway.'

'Well yes, I know, but living there permanently with Tim will be different . . . It'll make all the difference in the world.'

'To whom?' One slim hand dangled in the grass, her eyes had closed again, 'I suppose you mean to Tim and me?'

'Dal, I'm sorry . . . I wasn't being nosy.'

'It's all right, I don't mind telling you. You must have noticed during lunch that the conversation veered off Canada rather. You see, Tim getting this Canadian post matters not a jot to me.'

'But . . . ' I sat bolt upright in the

lounger, setting my feet in the grass.

'I'm not going to Canada. I'm staying right here in England.'

Silence fell between us. I was struck dumb by her words. A wasp zoomed by, then settled on a geranium, crawling over the warm velvety leaves.

'Do you mean you're staying here for always . . . you're never going to join Tim?'

'Maybe not.'

'Does Tim know?'

'Of course he knows. I had to tell him, he has his plans to make.'

'But Uncle Jocelyn said . . . ' I stopped and bit my lip, choosing my words with care. 'I thought you loved Canada, the Canadian way of life. I thought that was why you went there so often.'

'I prefer England now, particularly London. London's got everything . . . everything I want.' She too swung her feet on the grass and sat looking at me over the gap between our chairs, her face a few feet from mine. She was so very pretty at close range ... that peerless skin, the cameo features, the graceful way her neck was set on her shoulders. Tim must be distracted, he must be going mad. No wonder he was so short-tempered, quarrelling with Charles ... he must feel like quarrelling with the whole wide world.

'Oh Dal, couldn't you *try* it!'

She looked amused at my outburst, but I had to have my say. 'Couldn't you try it? I know how you feel. I mean I know that marriage isn't all ... isn't all it's ... '

'Cracked up to be?' She threw me a sidelong glance, then looked down at her dress, pleating the material with quick nervous movements, jangling the bracelets on her wrist. 'Nina ... tell me, what are your views on divorce?'

Her words went through me like a small electric shock. I heard myself catch my breath. 'I know nothing about it.'

'But are you against it ... on principle?'

'I don't know . . . how can you ask me that. But yes I rather think I am. I don't really think about it much.'

'Oh.'

'Are you in love with someone else . . . someone other than Tim?' My headache was real now, it streaked behind my eyes. Talking of divorce seemed to bring it very close . . . too close for comfort . . . too near the bone. Divorce . . . divorce . . . I loathed the sound of the word. How could Dal contemplate it . . . how could she possibly! She and Tim had been married for over five years!

'Yes, it's true that I'm in love with someone else. Clever Nina, right on target for once!'

There was something offensive about the way she said that and the pain in my head grew worse. In any case I couldn't sit and discuss a marriage breakdown . . . it was like having the dreaded enemy firing at one's gates.

'I'm going into the house, Dal. My head's shocking. I feel queasy. I must get out of the light.'

'Oh but sweetie, why didn't you say . . . a touch of the sun perhaps?' She looked at me obliquely out of those blue-green eyes. 'It *is* the sun, I suppose . . . there's nothing else wrong?'

'I'm not pregnant, if that's what you mean.'

'I didn't. I only just wondered if everything in the marriage field was going well for you.'

'Perfectly well, thank you.'

'You and Charles got married very suddenly, didn't you?'

We were in the house now, in the blessed cool of the lounge. I lay back and shut my eyes as the room began to go round.

'Pretty quickly, yes.' I wished she'd stop talking, expecting me to answer questions. I didn't intend to discuss Charles and me with Dal or anyone else. I wondered what Charles would say about Tim and Dal splitting up. Would Tim tell him whilst they were out this afternoon? It seemed pretty likely that he would.

We were just finishing tea when the two men returned and I could see at once they'd had their row out. The forked animosity that had previously flashed between them was replaced by an obvious yet refined form of 'sulks'. Charles came and sat by me, breathing heavily down his nose. Tim took his tea and cake and went outside by himself.

'Head any better, darling?' Charles took the cup that Dal held out to him and helped himself to sugar from the basin on the trolley.

'No it's not.' Dallas chimed in before I could reply. 'You really should look after her better, Charles.'

Charles didn't answer her, but looked 'daggers drawn'. Dallas grinned wickedly back.

'Charles and I,' I said slowly, 'prop each other up . . . it's a standard-type arrangement that works.'

'How sweet,' She smiled again, and I knew that *she* knew I was varnishing the truth, painting it rose-pink at that.

Good Lord, I thought, what a terrible visit. How right Charles was not to want to have them. How I wished I had taken his advice. But I couldn't possibly have known that things had gone this far; Charles should have warned me in advance. Actually he was often very reticent about his family, giving me the feeling that in spite of being his wife I was still not entitled to be told.

It was an inexpressible relief when, soon after six, the little red car went spuming down the drive, flinging out gravel on the lawns.

'Do go and lie down, Nina, you look all in.' Charles' brows were drawn together in a deep worried frown. His words were solicitous, but his tone was not. I knew he wanted to be on his own. Yet somehow I couldn't leave the matter just like that.

'Did Tim tell you about he and Dal . . . that she's not going to Canada after all?'

'Yes he did.'

'Is it serious, Charles? Do you think

they'll divorce? Does Tim mind . . . is he very upset?'

He swung round so quickly he trod on my foot. 'Of course he's upset . . . what a question to ask!'

'She's in love with someone else.'

'Well that's her problem. Now go and lie down, have a couple of hours' sleep. I'll bring you up something on a tray later on.'

So I went upstairs and lay on the bed, closing my eyes against the yellow evening light. I couldn't get the afternoon out of my thoughts. Dal's face, her hair, the way she moved her hand, slid across my mind's eye like a roll of film. 'You and Charles got married very suddenly, didn't you?' Now why should she say that . . . what was she implying? Of course she was right; we *had* got married suddenly . . . almost, one might say, in indecent haste, except that there'd been nothing indecent about it; we'd just been very much in love.

I could remember Charles' proposal

as if it were yesterday. I'd known him only a very short time ... I'd known him exactly a week. We'd met in a very unusual way too. Charles had been staying in Lemston on business, and I'd knocked him down in the car. He hadn't been hurt, only very slightly bruised, and I'd taken him back to the surgery at home and given him treatment for shock. I'd seen him every evening for a week after that. He proposed to me on the Friday, his last night in Lemston, over a leisurely dinner at The Swan. That was the evening I'd known I was in love with him, had known I was caught up, as inextricably bound, as a fly in a magic web.

'How old are you, Nina?' His words had come suddenly, making me jump.

'Twenty.'

'You're very young; I can top that by a good eight years.'

'Age is relative,' I'd assured him, confident that it was, 'and I'm old for my years, you know.'

'Your father thinks the world of you.'

'He's getting married again, to a widow in the town . . . to the widow of the doctor who died.'

'So I understand.'

'I shall get a job away from home. I may even emigrate.'

'Surely you needn't be quite so drastic . . . why emigrate for heaven's sake?'

'It'll be a change.'

'Why is every woman so mad about change?'

'Have you . . . known many women?'

'I knew one . . . very well. I hoped to marry her, but things didn't work out that way.'

'I'm sorry.'

'What would you say if I asked you to marry me?'

'What did you say!'

'Marry me Nina . . . *will* you marry me. We could be happy, I know we could. We could make a go of things.'

'But, Charles, it's only a week . . . '

'I don't care if it's a week, a day, or

only ten minutes. I'm not joking, I'm serious. I want you . . . I love you . . . I want to marry you!'

And that was how it had been.

Charles had been ardent in those days . . . ardent, impetuous, very loving. And as I got up from the bed and closed the window, the cataclysmic contrast between then and now hit me like a physical force. Where had it all gone . . . that spontaneous loving, and what did one do when it ebbed away, trickled away like the sands of time, till only the dregs were left.

As I sat at the dressing table and switched on the light . . . as I looked at my face in search of the truth, I was filled with a despair so deep and overwhelming I wanted to rush from the house.

5

Charles had mentioned when Tim and Dal were with us that he'd be going to Northumberland during the first week in July, so I wasn't too surprised when at the end of June he told me it had all been arranged.

'Why have you got to go?'

'To revise a client's portfolio of investments.'

'I thought stockbrokers dealt with those.'

'Occasionally lawyers advise their clients and work in liaison with the brokers themselves.'

'I see.'

I spread marmalade on my toast and viewed it with distaste. It was too hot to eat. The heatwave had lasted. Outside on the lawn the water-sprinkler rotated, making its creaking noise. 'How long will you be away?'

'Four days . . . leave here on Saturday, get back Tuesday night.' He put down his paper and looked at me worriedly. 'Nina, why don't you go and stay with your father? I'm not very happy about your being here on your own.'

'Can't I come with you?' The question seemed to drop like a pebble in a pool. Oh, Charles, say yes . . . say yes . . . say yes. We might come together again up in Northumberland; there might be something happen there that would just tip the scales. We'd been miles apart since that ghastly family party; any overtures I'd made had been to no avail . . . he was glassed in, walled up, shut right away . . . I simply couldn't reach him any more. So say yes, Charles . . . please, please say yes . . . don't turn me down this time.

'Oh darling, for goodness sake . . . ' the worried look left his face to be replaced by a patient one, 'it just wouldn't be sensible . . . it's simply not on. All that way and in this heat, and it isn't as if I'll be away for long. You couldn't stay with me at old Stewart's house. We'd have to find a room for you in the village somewhere, and Avonsdale's a tiny little place!'

'Oh.'

'You'd be bored stiff.'

'Not with you.'

'But that's the whole point . . . you wouldn't *be* with me. I'll be staying up at The Hall.'

'Oh all right . . . I see . . . I'm sorry to be stupid. But we are still going to Corfu in September?'

'Of course we are. What's that got to do with it? Now why don't you go and stay with your father. He'd be pleased as Punch to have you at home.'

'I'm not keen.'

'Don't you think it's time you stopped resenting your stepmother. She seems a very decent sort to me.'

'I don't resent her. I know she's decent. I'll go and stay with Estelle.'

'What?'

'With Estelle . . . you know at

Clayborough. There's lots to do there. I can swim in the river if this weather holds out and go into Windsor and shop. Estelle's always pleased to see me, we'll have a lot of fun. I might as well stay the whole week.'

'All right, if that's what you want.' He drained his cup, thrust his napkin into its ring and came round to kiss me goodbye. I returned his kiss absently, surprised he hadn't demurred, because I knew he didn't like Estelle much. He thought she was eccentric, which I suppose she is a bit. She's mother's younger sister and she writes plays and things. She's glamorous and dissipated and hard-boiled as well. I've always been fond of Estelle.

She seemed quite pleased when I telephoned her later to tentatively broach my plan.

'But my angel, how lovely! What a good idea!'

'It won't bother you, will it? I won't stop you writing?'

'No, to both questions. I'm dying to

see you. Get a taxi from the station, I'm afraid my car's in dock, but I'll be waiting for you at 'Willow Barn', arms outstretched!'

* * *

She wasn't though. When I paid off the taxi in the cart-track road, and made my way to 'Willow Barn' through the girdle of trees, there was no glamorous aunt on the veranda steps, not an outstretched arm to be seen. Instead there was a pencilled note sellotaped to the bell. 'Out of booze, gone to replenish, back half-twelve. E.'

I found the key in the usual place, unlocked the door and went inside. It was the same as it always was in Estelle's house . . . airy, a little dusty, fantastically still . . . nothing to be heard but the ticking of the clocks and the chugging and putt-putting of the launches on the river as they passed downstream to the lock.

Dumping my case in a corner of the

hall I decided to wait for Estelle outside. There was a seat at the river's edge and I ran down to it, sitting with my feet amongst the ducks. It was beautiful here, typically 'Wind in the Willows'. The willows, of course, gave the cottage its name . . . there were two very close to where I was sitting . . . drooping, delicate, trailing their 'skirts' in the water. Every now and then the breeze would whisk them up; they'd hang free for a second, then fall back in place, neatly like the folds of a dress.

I twisted round on the seat and looked back at the cottage. 'Willow Barn' wasn't large, but it was set in spacious grounds; this had the effect of making it a show-place with its colour-washed walls and lanky chimneys and its air of having sat there for years. The two main bedrooms were set in the roof, with their windows facing riverwards, of course. The river frontage, or mooring, had a wooden landing-stage. Estelle owned a motor cruiser, *Gay Gabriella* which was rocking at the landing-stage now.

Due to the noise and wash of a pleasure boat passing, I didn't hear Estelle till she was charging down the lawn.

'My angel . . . I'm so *sorry*, but I had to get stocked up . . . *so* inconvenient without the car!' She hugged me tightly and looked me up and down, whilst I stood and stared at her. She smelt dramatic, she looked dramatic in skin tight lemon pants, her hair massed extravagantly on top of her head. She's dark haired like me, and has the same kind of face. We're like my maternal grandmother, my mother was the same. Of course Estelle's in her forties, which makes a lot of difference, but she carries her years very well. She put an arm about my waist and we went towards the house. 'Lunch first, you must be starving, then an afternoon in the sun. It's lovely to see you, Nina, but how slim you are . . . I can span your waist with my hand.'

'I like being slim.'

'Brought your swimming things?'

'A scarlet bikini I bought up in Town.'

'You'll stop all the traffic on the river no doubt, and the men'll go on strike at the lock!'

'I hope not.'

'How's Charles?'

'Oh he's well . . . busy, but well.'

I felt her look at me but I stared straight ahead. I wasn't giving Estelle any clues.

'Do you good to have a few days apart . . . absence and the heart growing fonder, as they say. Do you like avocados stuffed with prawns?'

'Love them.'

'Set two trays then, we'll eat in the garden. All the food's cold, too hot to cook today. I thought we'd have a snack lunch then dinner in Windsor tonight. There's a hotel on the river that's out of this world.'

I sliced brown bread and butter and tipped strawberries into a dish. 'How will we go if we haven't got the car?'

'Darling, you're all behind . . . we're on a waterway, remember . . . we'll go in *Gay Gabriella* of course . . . we'll tootle upstream in style.'

I laughed, feeling happier. Estelle was a tonic; she was fun to be with. She reminded me of mother all over again . . . it was like having mother back. Over lunch, though, she told me some surprising news.

'I've bought a house in Brighton, Nina . . . a small terraced house in the old part of the town.'

'*Have* you?' I stopped eating my strawberries and looked at her in surprise.

'And I came across it in the oddest way. I was down there for a weekend, got bored with the crowd I was with, and walked on my own around the older part of Brighton.'

'You mean Kemp Town?'

'No, going up towards the station, to the right of Queen's Road. There are streets and streets of small terraced houses there . . . it's a shabby enough area, but fashionably so. Anyway, to cut a long story short, I found this little house next door to a pub. There was a For Sale card in the window with a phone number underneath. The pub was open, so in I went and rang the Johnny up.'

'But Estelle . . . were you intending to buy a house in Brighton?'

'I'd thought about it vaguely, not very seriously. But Nina, this is the really amazing thing . . . when I rang the number and spoke to the man, who do you think it was?'

'Sean Connery, no less?'

'It was Duncan Stevens!'

'What!'

'My step-nephew, your step-brother . . . one of the family no less!'

'But how incredible!'

'I thought you'd be surprised.'

'I met him on the Brighton train, some weeks back.'

'He told me. He wanted to know how you were . . . seemed very interested.'

'But did you know him . . . remember him?'

'But darling, of course! He was at your father's wedding. You don't think I'd have forgotten such a gorgeous chunk of man?'

'I had.'

'Oh well you . . . you've got your head in the clouds! But to get back to my story, it seemed that Duncan was acting for the owner of the cottage, a man called Bertram Lee. Mr. Lee's an arthritic, couldn't manage the stairs. He lives in a nursing-home on the sea front now; Duncan seems to help him out.'

'He seems to help a lot of people.' I remembered the holiday aunt.

'He's an absolute sweetie, there's no doubt about it. Now where was I . . . oh yes, I went to see the house, liked it, made an acceptable offer, the lawyers got cracking, and now it's mine . . . all bar settling a price for the furniture which I would like to have as well. Now how about that for quick, decisive action!'

'Will you be selling 'Willow Barn'?'

'No, I'm too fond of it. You forget darling that writers are a movable feast. I shall live here from May to end of September, at Brighton from October round to May. In other words I shall summer here, winter there. I can't stand coastal resorts at the height of the season; during the winter they're heaven . . . acres of promenade, wind-swept, gale-lashed, not a living soul in sight!'

'Except little old ladies and men with dogs.'

'Well those, of course.'

'I must say it all sounds . . . lovely Estelle.' She was having the effect, as she so often did, of taking my breath away. 'And I suppose it is pretty eerie here in the winter?'

'You're telling me . . . when the mists creep up the river and the trees are bare . . . ugh!'

'There'll be mists at Brighton.'

'Yes, but homely ones . . . anyway they're sea fret, not mists. And there's the theatre and decent cinemas, restaurants galore . . . it'll suit me down to the ground. So there you are my pet, if you and Charles want a holiday by the sea, you can have the wee house whenever I'm not there. I'll make sure and give you the key.'

'Thank you.'

'Don't look so gloomy . . . I do mean it, you know.'

'Charles is always so busy Estelle. I doubt if I'd ever get him down to Brighton. If we manage to stick to our Corfu date, it's just about as much as we will.'

'That's men for you . . . work first, wife and home second, it seems. Still you could go, get a break from routine . . . self-preservation and all that.'

'When you're married you have to preserve your man as well.'

'What's that supposed to mean?'

'You can't just leave him to get on with it on his own. Charles will be at it all this weekend . . . sorting out some old man's investments.'

'I suppose he has to make these efforts whilst he's young.'

'But he *is* a partner; he's reached his goal, his perch if you like . . . no one can knock him off that.'

'Well you don't know, do you . . . ' Estelle halved a peach and slung the stone in the river, 'business, even professional business, is a very chancy thing. Still I don't think you need worry about 'our Charles' . . . he'll strive and be successful, come hell or high water; his jib's the right cut for it, his hair the right colour. Oh, by the way, changing the subject, how's my brother in-law?'

'Father? Oh fine. He and Val seem very happy.'

'Of course Valerie had been a doctor's wife before.'

'Yes.'

'I wonder if her husband was as dedicated as John.'

'They think a lot of father at Lemston, so he must make a pretty worthy successor.'

'They thought a lot of him at

Fawding, everyone adored him, except for the ghastly little Morrison man.'

'I don't remember a Morrison man.'

'Oh darling, of course you do . . . the one who came along in the middle of the night and shied a brick through the surgery. I was staying with you at the time . . . you *must* remember. There was a fearful shindig. Morrison went berserk, threatened to wreck the place. It was because his wife had died. He accused your father of neglect. It was nonsense of course . . . John never neglected a patient in the whole of his life, but there was a terrible fuss . . . I was scared stiff . . . Mary and I hid under the stairs!'

'Yes I *do* remember . . . although it was ages ago. I'd have been about fifteen, sitting for my 'O' Levels. Yes, I remember, it's all coming back. Father got lots of anonymous letters and there was something about it in the Press. Poor daddie . . . being a doctor isn't all power and prestige. I think mother got very fed up with it sometimes. She wasn't a *born* doctor's wife.'

'Too true, she wasn't. She was like me . . . enjoyed variety, moving around. Anyway, that's enough of this serious talk . . . let's change into our swimsuits, have an hour on the bank, followed by a long hard swim.'

★   ★   ★

I'd forgotten the delights of swimming in river water . . . the weighty coldness, the patches of warmth, the drag of the current, one's body slicing through . . . floating face upwards, staring at the sky . . . the clouds, the blueness, the gloom under the trees . . . then turning face down again, making for the bank . . . the alarm of the ducks, the disdain of the swans, and the wonderful, marvellous feeling of well-being, of being suspended, of this being all . . . the trees and the sky and the sour river smell, the coldness and the patches of warmth. Oh Charles, oh Charles, of *course* I love you, but there are other things as well.

And because of the 'other things' I was able to relax, even if I were only marking time.

On Sunday our day followed much the same pattern, then came Monday and the postman and Estelle all perturbed.

'Nina, I'm terribly sorry, I've got to go up to Town!' She came into my room with a letter in her hand, a pair of enormous spectacles askew on her nose, 'I've heard from the TV people ... they want me to sit in on a conference ... I may be up there all day! Oh darling ... how awful ... I hope you don't mind, but I'm afraid I'll have to go!'

'Of course you must go, and of course I don't mind!' I got out of bed and pulled on my robe, 'I'll go and get breakfast; now don't worry about me, I'll be perfectly happy lazing about. And this afternoon I'll make a pizza to have with our supper, and get in some more of that wine.'

'Lovely!' She looked at me owlishly over the top of her glasses. I had a feeling I'd not heard all. 'There's just one thing . . . '

'Oh?'

'Duncan Stevens is coming.'

'What *here*?' I wheeled in the doorway, stubbing my toe. 'Coming here, all the way from Brighton, but Estelle . . . whatever for?'

'Not from Brighton, from Windsor. He's staying there with friends, friends in his line of business, I understand. And he's coming to settle the price of the furniture . . . the furniture in the Brighton house. You remember I told you he was acting for Mr. Lee. I'd like the whole lot, exactly as it stands. We were going to negotiate a deal.'

'You didn't tell me Duncan was at Windsor.'

'Didn't I? I thought I did. He rang me up last week . . . we fixed the meeting then.'

'I see.'

'Nina . . . you've gone quite pale

119

. . . are you feeling all right?'

'Yes.'

'He's due this afternoon, but of course I'll put him off. There's no point in him coming if I'm not here.'

'None at all.' I sliced bread with rapid strokes and switched on the toaster. I got out butter and jam.

'Unless . . . ' there was a moment of silence broken by the toaster which was one of the pop-up kind, 'Unless you felt you could see him for me. Would it be too much to ask? I can give you the top price I'm prepared to pay, leave a signed cheque for you to fill in. Of course don't give him exactly what he asks at first . . . it's business after all.'

'I can haggle.' I turned round and smiled at her . . . I felt rather pleased, 'I can haggle, I'm good at it . . . even Charles says so . . . full of Eastern promise and all that!'

'You'll do it then?'

'Of course. When's he coming?'

'Three o'clock, and he's very unlikely

to be late; he's going back to Brighton tonight.'

After Estelle had bounced off in the local taxi, I changed into my swimsuit and made for the bank, stepping down the iron rung ladder into the water, gasping as it rose up my trunk. I could never quite bring myself to dive headfirst in; I felt I might get stuck in the mud.

I struck out from the bank and swam steadily up-stream, trying to perfect 'the crawl'. When my arms were leaden, my chest fit to burst, I trod water gently, and turned about, letting the current carry me back to 'Willow Barn', scarcely needing to move a limb. As I got within sight of our lanky chimneys, I was considerably startled to see a man on the lawn, a tall broad-shouldered man with bright fair hair, wearing a bright blue shirt. Good Lord, I thought, it's Duncan Stevens . . . Estelle must have muddled up the time.

I felt ridiculously self-conscious as I pulled myself up the steps and stood wet and dripping on the wooden landing stage, snatching off my cap. My hair fell heavy and damp to my shoulders; I shook it clear of my eyes.

'Hullo, how nice to see you.' Even my voice sounded wet.

He came towards me smiling, stepping lightly over the boards. He had the movements of an athlete, quick and spare.

'I'm early. Does it matter?'

'Of course not . . . not at all.' We walked together to the rustic seat, and I grabbed at my wrap, thrusting my arms in the wide towelling sleeves, drawing the broad belt tight. He watched me gravely as I dried my face on the large cotton hanky he held out.

'Your aunt rang me from the station. She said you were here and would be acting for her. I asked if it would be all right for me to come this morning. She said I'd probably find you swimming in the river.'

'Which you did of course!'

'Which I did! You swim well. I'd been

watching you for some time. River swimming's difficult . . . the water doesn't give.'

'It's like swimming in mercury going upstream.' I hesitated on the veranda steps . . . what would it be best to do first? 'Perhaps . . . ' I suggested, 'you'd like some coffee. Then we could settle the figures as well. I'm just a little nervous of acting for my aunt. She looks easy-going but she's right on the ball, particularly where money's concerned.'

'*And* we're on opposite sides of the fence!'

'Which is why I'm nervous!'

We laughed together and I went upstairs to dress, putting on white linen slacks. I'd got very brown, my skin looked polished . . . I hoped I looked my best.

'When I rang your aunt last week, she didn't say you were coming,' said Duncan when I joined him in the hall.

'I don't suppose she knew then . . . it was arranged all at once. Charles had to go away on business; he didn't want me to be at home on my own.'

'You couldn't go with him then?'

'It wasn't possible.'

We went into the kitchen and he stood in the doorway, looking out at the trees.

'What a charming house this is.'

I switched on the percolator and put a pan of milk on the stove. 'Yes, isn't it. Yet a lot of it's the setting. If it were in an ordinary suburban road, it wouldn't look anything like this. Here, with the trees and the lawns and the river, it becomes . . . well almost unique.'

He had turned back into the room and was looking straight at me. Something in his eyes made me tear my own away and stare at the milk which had reached the frothy stage. I moved it a little on one side.

'It's a setting that becomes you. You must be a river girl.'

'Well thank you for those kind words, but I latch on to any environment . . . blend with the grass . . . maybe I'm a chameleon at heart!'

He flushed and I wished I'd been a little less derisive. I pushed his coffee at him and rattled out some biscuits, suggesting that we eat them in the little morning room and went through the furniture list as well. Arguing over the figures, getting down to business, dissolved the embarrassment, lightened the atmosphere, made us both more relaxed. I was pleased with myself because I came out on top . . . £40 to the good. Duncan laughed as I made out Estelle's cheque and handed it over to him. 'Full marks . . . you should be in business with me.'

'I doubt if I could keep it up for long. I'm very much flash in the pan!'

'When are you coming to Brighton again?'

'Oh I don't know. We aren't going to live there. Charles' firm changed their plans.'

'Do you mind?'

'I can bear it. Duncan, what's

Estelle's house like? It *was* the one Leila mentioned in the train? When Estelle mentioned a Bertie Lee, I remembered at once that your aunt had said . . . '

'It's the same house, yes.'

'But what a coincidence!'

'Not such a great one. There aren't so many properties up for sale now. Still I suppose it was a coincidence she was looking just there. It must, as they say, have been meant!'

'Tell me about it.' We were walking in the orchard, Duncan with head bent, mainly to avoid the trees. 'Tell me about it,' I pressed, as we came full circle and sat down on the river seat again.

'It's about one hundred and fifty years old, tall, thin, white, 2-bedroomed, built on three levels.'

'Has it got a garden?'

'A tiny walled one at the back . . . it's a split level house. The front door opens straight onto the street.'

'Would I like it?'

'I think you'd love it, providing you

didn't mind a warehouse opposite and the station only a stone's throw away. I thought of buying it for myself at one time, but all in all I think I'm better where I am. And actually I may not always be in Brighton . . . I'm contemplating a move of some kind.'

An enormous barge passed, making a harsh stuttering sound . . . it had 'Gritting Works' painted on its side. We watched it grind past, making a churn of foamy wake.

'I wish I could ask you to have lunch with me,' Duncan's hand grazed mine as it lay on the seat, 'but these friends at Windsor have arranged something special and I'm going back to Brighton just before tea.'

'Oh that's all right. I didn't expect . . .'

'Will you be going home to see your father soon? I wondered if we might perhaps arrange something together. I go fairly often to see my mother. It is, if you remember, our mutual home now . . . or our mutual parental home.'

'I don't go much.'

'Why?'

'Oh, Duncan, what a question. I don't know how to answer it. Partly because I can't leave Charles and partly because I feel awkward with your mother . . . I'm sorry, but there it is.'

'It's an awkwardness that could be easily overcome. I don't think you've tried very hard.'

'Well really . . . '

'Try with me, Nina. I'll help you. I know how you feel. It was difficult for me at first, but it's worse for a girl . . . between a girl and her mother there's a very special link.'

'Did *you* mind when your mother . . . when Valerie married father?'

'Of course.'

'Well I don't see *why*! Father's a good catch!'

'So's my mother.'

I went very pink, then started to laugh; so, to my relief, did he. 'Oh

Duncan, we're on opposite sides of the fence *again*!'

'We needn't be. That's not what I want. What I'd really like . . . '

'Well go on, I'm all intrigued. You can't stop there!'

'I'd better. It's getting late. I'll have to go.' He moved away from me on the seat and I wondered if I'd offended him. We'd been on tricky ground talking about our parents. I was sorry if he were annoyed because it was lovely to have a step-brother. I didn't want to fall out with him quite so soon.

Yet I couldn't think of a single thing to say as we walked through the back gate and the beech trees and the aspens, out to the cart-track road. His car was parked there, the cream estate car, the one I'd seen at Fawding, had ridden in to the station . . . it seemed a long time ago now.

'It's all meeting and parting.' He put a hand on my shoulder, then backed towards the car. 'I'm sorry to rush away like this.'

'Think nothing of it! I quite understand!'

'I wonder if you do,' was what I thought he said, as he let in the clutch and the car moved off, bumping over the rough hewn road.

6

Duncan's visit unsettled me. I didn't sleep that night. Lying wakeful in the darkness I knew the 'marking time' was over. I must take up the cudgels of married life again, get back to where I belonged. Charles would be at 'High Walls' tomorrow evening; that's when I would be there.

The decision was made, yet sleep still eluded me, and I got out of bed and drew the curtain on one side. Estelle was in the summerhouse, working on a script. She always worked there, never in the house. I could see the lighted window, hear the rattle of the type-writer, the occasional ping of the bell. It was a funny time to be there, in the small hours of the morning, but Estelle worked whenever the urge was upon her, and she'd come back full of 'urge' last night. How lucky people were who had creative work . . . something that no one could touch or interfere with . . . something that belonged to oneself.

I opened the window and leaned right out, breathing in the night. It was dark, but not quite dark, there was a strip of moon, and as my eyes grew accustomed to the meagre light I could make out the ducks fast asleep on the bank, their beaks screwed into their backs. There was a fisherman camped on the opposite bank, with his hurricane lamp and folding stool and hat like Sherlock Holmes. I heard him shift and cough as he re-cast his line, saw the flare of his match as he set it to his pipe. I looked up, the sky was streaking, soon it would be light; the sun would rise, the river would colour, the fisherman would get up and go.

Estelle was surprised when I took in her breakfast and told her I was going home.

'What on earth for! You've only just come . . . I thought you were here for a week.'

'Charles will be home today.'

'So what?'

'I want to be there.'

She gave me a long straight look over the rim of her cup.

'There's nothing wrong, is there Nina, between you and Charles?'

'Of course not.'

'Because if there is, have it out with him. Don't let it go on. *If* there's something wrong get to the root of it fast ... don't let it grow into a whacking great tree that you can't do anything about.'

'There's nothing wrong Estelle.'

'All right ... if you say so.'

She knew there was, of course. Estelle's no fool, she observes people closely, but there was no point whatever in confiding in her. And even if I'd admitted to there being something wrong, what I couldn't have explained was that it doesn't always do to have things out on the mat. It may work in theory but in practice it does not. Talking doesn't always iron problems out, sometimes it makes them more important and larger . . . sometimes it make them worse. And without being unfair to Estelle, she was out of her depth. She was single so she couldn't know how difficult it was for a husband and wife to discuss together their marriage which seemed to be heading for the rocks. They didn't want to face the true state of affairs . . . they just wanted to keep jogging through each day hoping that things would improve. I knew that Charles would loathe prodding it over . . . failure was anathema to him.

Estelle was quiet all through breakfast and just before I went she slipped the key of her Brighton house into my shoulder bag.

'Well, there's your escape route, just in case you need one.'

'I hope I shan't. But I'd like to see the house. I may go down for the day some time.'

'The address is on the label — 23 Forge Lane.'

'O.K. I'll remember that.'

By half past eleven I was in the London train, speeding through the factory chimneys of Slough, drawing into Paddington, crossing to London Bridge, my thoughts already turning towards the shopping I must do . . . steak for supper, fresh fruit, a carton of cream, some of that long French bread. 'You're feeding the brute,' said my cynical self, 'trying to soften him up'. Well, so what . . . why shouldn't I . . . I'd try every route, and if the way to Charles' heart was through his stomach then that was the way I'd take.

I walked the short distance from the station to 'High Walls'. My case wasn't heavy, and for some strange reason I didn't want to reach home too soon. Having pushed myself here I was now lagging back, like the boy who walked unwillingly to school. But Charles wouldn't be home until six o'clock at earliest . . . it was too soon to start 'butterflies' now.

'The Larches', 'The Limes', 'The Cedars', 'The Elms' . . . then the gates of 'High Walls' which to my surprise were open . . . the Volvo was parked just inside. Charles . . . so he was home . . . he'd got here early. Anticipation sparked me now . . . I cut across the lawn, the french windows were open, I'd go in that way . . . he was most likely having some tea.

I heard the sound of voices when I was halfway over the grass. Charles must have a visitor . . . how annoying that was . . . how maddening to get home and find someone here. My feet slowed, almost stopped as I worked out who it was. I strained my ears, I walked with stealth. I came to a halt ouside the window when the voices flowed clearly out.

'In my own house . . . I'm damned if I will! Haven't you any decency, Dal?'

There was a tinkling laugh which I recognised instantly. For the life of me I couldn't move from the spot.

'Trusting little Neenie . . . she'd

never cotton on. Why ever did you marry her Charles?'

'I might ask why you married Tim, when you happened to belong to me!'

'You know why, darling . . . for economic reasons. And at least I got *something* out of my marriage. You got nothing but a coltish girl who can't even give you a child.'

'What a cold-blooded bitch you are!'

'A bitch maybe . . . but not cold-blooded . . . as well you know!'

'Shut up!'

'And I could give you a child, you know, practically at the drop of a hat. We could even get married with a bit of re-arranging . . . a few legal chores which you know all about.'

'You talk about marriage as though it's a game of chess. I'm married to Janina . . . you're married to Tim. And that, so far as I am concerned, is the way it's going to stay.'

'Whatever your inclinations may be?'

'Yes.'

'How frightfully noble of you!'

I did move then. I moved involuntarily forward. I crossed the threshold, stepped into the room, and stood there blinking stupidly at the scene that met my eyes.

Charles was standing by the fireplace, one elbow on the shelf. Dal, shoes off, was full-length on the couch, head flung back so that her hair draped the arm. She moved not a quarter of an inch when she saw me, except for her lips, which parted a little, showing her small even teeth. Charles' arm came off the mantelshelf, and he stared at me white-faced. I felt a second's pity for him, superseded by fury . . . how *dare* he bring her into our house!

'Will you please go, Dal?' My voice was off-beat, but at least it was steady. Charles stepped forward and gripped me by the arm. Perhaps he thought I was going to spring at Dal, do her some mortal harm. He needn't have worried, I couldn't have touched her. To me, at that moment, she had the repulsion of a snake. I couldn't have scratched her with a pin.

'Well, well, well . . . look who's dropped in!' She swung her legs to the floor, slid her feet into sandals, looking at me with limpid eyes and a face so beautiful that once again I had a fleeting sympathy for Charles.

'Your handbag is here.' I pushed it with my shoe, and as she bent to retrieve it I saw the faintest of flushes tinge the pearl of her skin.

'My case is in the car, Charles.' She spoke to him, but looked at me, undisguised triumph in her smile. Her words lunged home like the point of a knife. Her case . . . the car . . . she'd been to Northumberland with Charles. She knew him well . . . she'd known him a long time . . . before she'd married Tim . . . long before me. Dal was the girl Charles had hoped to marry . . . Charles was the man Dal was in love with. But Dal had married Tim, Charles had married me . . . I had jumped joyously into the gap she had

139

left . . . the gap I'd been unable to fill.

'You've got a lot to learn, Nina . . . ' she wasn't finished yet, she gave the knife a final twist . . . 'the thing is have you got the gumption to learn it, or have you left it too late?'

'That's enough, Dal!' Charles' arm came round my shoulders, he put me in a chair. 'I'll take Dal to the station . . . you wait for me here.' I nodded, said nothing. I felt rather sick. Sweat broke out on my body, I felt it trickling between my breasts. He shouldn't have done it . . . he shouldn't have done it . . . he couldn't do this to me! Then I looked at Dal and my heart seemed to stop . . . thu-ump . . . thu-ump . . . thu-ump . . . My chest ached, felt fit to burst, I couldn't get my breath . . . then it rushed in like gas and I gasped and coughed. I hoped that perhaps I might choke to death . . . I hoped that perhaps I might die. Instead I just sat there looking at Dal. Her dress was blue in some sort of linen. It was creased round the hem and at the back where she'd lain. Her very dishevelment was an enhancement of her sex, or it would be, I knew, to a man.

I watched them go out and cross the lawn . . . at least three feet apart. The very distance between them seemed proof of their closeness . . . Charles and Dal . . . Charles and Dal . . . Charles and Dal. She laughed when they reached the edge of the lawn . . . a high-pitched laugh of deliberate merriment, swiftly decapitated by the slam of the car door. What a fool I was, what a perfect fool, not to have realised before. Tim had known, of course he had known. He had laughed at me that Sunday on the lawn . . . when ignorance is bliss . . . and Dal had called him 'wet'. Surely he minded, but of course he did, I remembered his quarrel with Charles. And Uncle Joce had known, I was sure of it now. That was the reason why he'd got Tim the job abroad; he'd known about Charles and Dal. He'd probably seen them in London, seen them around together. Charles had been afraid Uncle Joce would 'blow'; that's why he hadn't wanted me to lunch with him that day.

All the pieces fitted now, the puzzle was complete. There'd been a lot of pieces and they'd been puzzling in themselves . . . Charles' evasiveness, his edginess, his swings of mood . . . a different sort of pattern to the way we made love. I might have known . . . I *should* have known . . . I ought to have suspected something. And to think that I'd thought it might be Charles' work that was making him so difficult to understand.

My legs went weak, I sank down on the pouffe. I was still wet and cold, my hands slipped together, as though palmed in grease. I stumbled over to the cocktail cabinet and poured myself a brandy, tossing it back like a hardened soak, feeling it fire my throat. It didn't matter if I were drunk . . . what did it matter. And when the blur wore off I wished it were back . . . anything was better that this pain of betrayal which bumped like a tooth in my chest.

But I was angry as well, and anger always helps. I crossed to the mirror and stared at my reflection . . . a brown polished face, with Russian-type cheek-bones, a wide mouth, dark eyes, pencil black brows. Not such a bad face, and I *had* been called beautiful . . . Charles had thought so when we first got married. A coltish girl was how *she* had described me . . . a coltish girl who couldn't give him a child. Well sucks to her . . . who wants a child . . . who wants a child when one's marriage is cracking . . . *had* cracked from side-to-side.

When I heard the car wheels on the gravel outside, the bang of the door, the sound of his footsteps, I panicked but only for a flying second. I kept standing up, I felt better that way . . . better to stand than sit in a crisis when the sense of danger is strong. And I was afraid of Charles, I realised that now. I had probably been afraid of him all along.

He looked at me once then looked away. He went over to the cabinet and took a cigarette from the box. He waved the box at me.

'Want one?'

'No thank you.'

'Do we *have* to stand!'

'No.'

I sat, he sat, and then he began . . . drawing on his cigarette so hard and long it had a perpetually red end.

'I'm sorry you had to find out like that.'

'You should have told me about her.'

'I tried to, many times. I found it impossible.'

'I mean you should have told me before we married. You should have told me she was the girl you'd once lived with.'

'Would you have married me if I had?'

'If I'd known it was Dal . . . no probably not.'

'Then that's your answer. And remember this, Nina, Tim and Dal were happily married at the time you and I got engaged. There was complete severance of . . . relationship between Dale and me.'

'I see.'

'Even so I intended to tell you about it eventually . . . when I felt things were right, when we were sure of one another, when we'd grown so close you couldn't misunderstand.'

'That closeness never came.'

'It came and went. We had it at first. I agree it's minimal now.'

His face had shuttered and his words roughly spoken were a death knell to my very last hope. But what had I hoped . . . what could I hope for? Perhaps I'd hoped he'd refute what I'd said. Perhaps I'd hoped he'd say he didn't love Dal, that the resumption of their affair was a one-night flip; that she meant nothing more to him than that. I suppose I wanted him to sweep me into his arms, vow undying love like the heroes in old films. But old films aren't real life, their heroes aren't real men, so Charles just sat there stiff and unyielding, jutting out his chin. I looked at him and hated him and the hate was a hardness . . . I could actually feel the hardness creeping up. He was sitting on the couch, the couch where Dal had lain. The cushions were still dented with the pressure of her body . . . erotic pictures formed and circled in my mind . . . the thought of her made me inflame.

'You were together in Northumberland.'

'It wasn't what I intended.'

'You'll be telling me next you weren't even there. You weren't staying up at The Hall at all, were you . . . you were in the village with her, making love to her . . . evidently there *was* room at the inn.'

'Don't be clever-clever Nina, it doesn't suit you.'

'But *you were there*?'

'Do you want a blow-by-blow account?'

'I can fill in the gaps very nicely, thank you. And it may surprise you to know it isn't so much that you slept with her that maddens me, it's that you brought her here . . . here to *our* home . . . you were going to . . . '

'I was *not*! There was absolutely no question . . . if you'd listened a bit harder, or a bit longer . . . '

'You were discussing me . . . having me over with her! I heard you!'

'If you'd stayed with Estelle until the end of the week you'd never have known a thing.'

'And that would have made it right, of course!'

'It would have been an end of the matter . . . once and for all!'

'Would it . . . would it . . . I don't believe you!' How dare he . . . how dare he . . . how dare he bring her here. 'You must think I'm naïve Charles . . . you must think I'm green. You're not going to tell me that your weekend in Northumberland was nothing but a clearing-up shower. And if it were . . . if it was . . . why bring her here . . . why bring her into this house! You didn't have to do it . . . you didn't *have* to do it

. . . and if I didn't matter what about Tim? How could you do that to your own brother? I thought there was some code of honour between brothers!'

We were both on our feet now . . . shock, restraint, finer feelings, respect, had all gone hurtling to the wall. The gloves were off, the masks were down . . . truth that pitiless destroyer of affinity licked around the room like lightning in a storm . . . spurring us on to make a kill.

'Tim took her from me in the first place don't forget!'

'But you weren't married to her . . . he wasn't stealing a wife!'

'I wanted to marry her more than life itself!'

'Pity she didn't feel the same.'

The silence that followed was too terrible to bear; a tense, taut silence, tangible too, like a stretched and over-stretched band. I broke it in desperation and my words came twanging back . . . they seemed to flick me in the face.

'We must separate, Charles. It's the

only thing to do. I've . . . I've been thinking about it for quite some time.'

'I know you have. You've made it very obvious.'

'I'm sorry.'

'We seem to have pulled on separate wires. I'll move out. It's easier for me.'

I bit my lip, feeling anger rising again. Of course it was easier for him. He'd go to her . . . I was making it easy . . . driving him into her arms. Well let him go then . . . let him go. If that's what he wanted let him jolly well have it . . . pointless to live as a wife with a man who hankered after someone else.

'I shall go to Estelle's I shan't stay here.'

'Perhaps that would be best.'

He was amenable now, agreeing with me. He wasn't protesting or exploding, there was relief on his face which had previously been white and drawn. My voice thickened I pushed past him, ran across the hall to the stairs.

'I'll get packed. I'll take all I can possibly carry. I'll send for the rest later on.'

'All right,' His calm was infuriating, I loathed him for it.

'Perhaps . . . ' I said evenly, 'you'll ring for a taxi . . . one from the rank will do.'

His reserve cracked at that; his face flushed darkly; he moved towards the stairs. As I ran up them he stepped close against my heels, turning me round on the upstairs landing, pushing me back against the rails.

'Like hell I will!' He shook me violently back and forth . . . back and forth like a doll . . . 'You can leave if you like . . . get away if you like, but I'll not help you . . . you can get your own vehicle. You seem to think I'm made of bloody indiarubber . . . I do have *some* feelings you know!'

I heard the front door crash as I got the cases out of the wardrobe. Running to the window I saw him striding down the road . . . legs and arms flailing, head flung back, as though he were pushing against a gale.

7

It was like being plunged into an alien world. I knew I wasn't dreaming, I knew it was real, and reality was a nightmare that went on and on.

During the first two weeks I was at Estelle's house I was petrified from morning till night.

I was constantly in suspense . . . would Charles come? I had an outsize conscience which made life hell. I slept only fitfully, I couldn't eat proper meals; even going to the shops required a superhuman effort. Washing and dressing and combing my hair was a toil and moil of its own.

The nights were the worst. They always are, of course. I'd wake in the small hours with a frantic sort of feeling; not fright exactly, just a terrible feeling at finding myself alone. It was a realisation that stunned me; it made me act stupidly. I'd listen for breathing, I'd stretch over the bed . . . nothing but coldness, an expanse of sheet; no coughs, no snorts, no masculine grunts, not even an unyielding back. And at three o'clock in the morning, waking up to this, I'd long to be back with Charles . . . in any 'kind of weather' . . . in any kind of mood . . . anything was better than this. But in the morning I'd know better . . . it was different then. In the cold light of day when logic's at its best, I'd know it was impossible to live with a man who wanted somebody else.

I wrote to my father and told him we had separated. I also wrote to Estelle. The latter wrote to say that Charles had telephoned to Clayborough, expecting I was staying with her there. 'I've given him your address, Nina, there was nothing else I could do. He'll have to know anyway, sometime or other, you can't hole up there for evermore.' Hard on the heels of that came a letter from the Bank to say that an account had been opened for me in Brighton and giving me the address of the Branch; 'Perhaps you would be good enough to call in sometime, in order that the arrangements made by Mr. Redman may be implemented forthwith.'

My hands shook a little as I folded the thick paper. Charles was running true to form looking after the business side. Nevertheless I'd get my own money transferred to the account. I wouldn't touch his unless I absolutely had to. In the meantime I'd get myself a job.

I was surprised when father arrived at the cottage — surprised and pleased, I nearly wept on his neck. I hadn't expected him to come, neither had I expected him to take my part. I thought he'd blame me and state his views, and try to pack me back to Charles like a parcel in the post. Father is terribly, terribly, straitlaced. He abhors divorce and abortion and promiscuity . . . he's only just got used to the pill.

'You married too quickly, Nina. I had my doubts at the time. That annoying old proverb has some truth in it, you know.'

'Marry in haste, repent at leisure. Clichés don't help me much now.'

'I'm sorry, old lady, but you'll have to face up to it. Charles is a decent chap; he has many excellent points, but you were never suited; you were poles apart in the way you looked at life. It's no good marrying in the white heat of attraction; you need to be compatible in basic ways. All this flim flam about love at first sight belongs to women's magazines. You've got to be good friends as well as lovers . . . have the same interests, view life the same way. You've got to have a good solid wall of affection to lean on when things get rough.'

'I expect you're right.'

'Now Val and I have talked it over, dear. We want you to come home and live. If you wanted a job you could soon get fixed up; they're always wanting secretaries at the medical centre . . . can't get enough help there. And there's the hospital at King's Lynn . . . there'd be no end to your scope.'

The chair he was sitting on had very slender legs. I heard it give an ominous creak.

'Oh I don't know . . . ' I began, 'I don't think . . . '

'Well at least come home until this trouble's over.'

Supposing he broke the chair . . . what would Estelle say . . . it was one of the expensive ones.

'What do you mean,' I said, trying to marshal my thoughts, 'what do you mean by 'until this trouble's over'?'

'What do I mean? I mean what I say . . . you and Charles intend to separate legally . . . or have I got it wrong?'

'We haven't discussed it.'

'Then you'd better get down to it . . . make a firm decision . . . no sense in having a lot of loose ends. Is Charles making provision for you? Have you had any money?'

'He pays some into a bank account here.'

'That's what I would have expected of him. Nina, I don't want to delve in matters that don't concern me, but presumably . . . I'm supposing . . . there's another woman?'

'Something like that.'

'Well either there is or there isn't.'

'All right father, there is.'

'Then come home to Val and me. You can't put up with that sort of thing. Come home to us darling . . . we'll sort it all out.'

'No . . . I must be here. I . . . I quite like it here. I want to remain on neutral ground.'

'I dare say you do, and I see what you mean, but you're not used to coping with things on your own.'

'I can learn.'

'Get Duncan to help you . . . yes, that's it . . . get Duncan . . . '

'Father! Another man isn't going to help me solve my marriage problems. I like Duncan, I think he's great, but I must manage on my own.'

'He's your step-brother, don't forget

. . . one of the family . . . a bit different from just being 'another man'.'

'I'd rather not involve him.'

Father looked perplexed and worried, but he argued very little after that. 'Well at least come to Lemston for a weekend soon,' was his final admonishment before he left to catch his train.

★ ★ ★

Uncle Joce arrived in a thunderstorm, plunging into Estelle's narrow little hall, shaking himself like a well-bred mastiff all over the parquet floor. He had heard the news, he said, quite by chance. He had met Miss Sanderson in Fortnums one lunch-time; she had given him a hint, which he had quickly followed up . . . it hadn't taken him long to cotton on.

'I didn't know you knew Estelle?' I made him some tea; he'd arrived at four o'clock. I wondered how I'd ever manage to hide the true facts from him

. . . Charles would be furious if he knew.

'I met her at your wedding . . . attractive woman . . . you'll be like her one day. Now my dear . . . what's all this tomfoolery about? And why are you living in this titivated rabbit hutch?' He looked around the lounge in disgust.

'Charles and I decided it would be best to live apart.'

'Nonsense . . . absolute nonsense . . . a futile conclusion! The longer these little rifts go on the harder they are to mend.'

Evidently Uncle Joce shared Estelle's views . . . they must have talked about us a lot.

'An onlooker sometimes sees most of the game,' he said as if reading my thoughts.

I went very red and didn't reply. He wolfed another slice of toast.

'Oil on troubled waters, my dear . . . that's what's needed. Now I may be an old man . . . an old widower to boot, but I've got eyes in my head, a very long memory, and what I don't know I can guess at . . . guess at pretty accurately. It's Tim's wife, isn't it . . . it's Dal?'

'She has to do with it.' I managed at last, controlling my emotions by going absolutely rigid and staring at the opposite wall.

'Thought so . . . *knew* so.'

'Uncle Joce . . . I know you mean well, but it's between Charles and me. Only we can decide what's best to do.'

'Talked about it have you? He's been down here, has he?'

'No, not . . . not yet.'

'Then it's time he did come . . . high time. I shall tell him so too!'

'Oh no, don't do that! Please don't do that! Please let things be. It's partly my fault that he hasn't been anyway. I forgot to leave him my address.'

'He knows it now, doesn't he?'

'Yes he does, but . . . '

'Be quiet girl . . . let me get on!' He looked so like the chairman thumping the table for order, that I found myself subsiding at once. 'He'll come anyway, whether I tell him to or not . . . he'll come for the sake of his job . . . Rudgleys like their partners to have tidy private lives.'

'I see.'

'But you don't, that's the whole point. A lot of background needs filling in. You young people go about things in quite the wrong way. Charles should have told you the whole story before you ever got wed.'

'It's not always easy to talk about these things.'

'It's nevertheless vital to clear the decks. Charles and Dallas were as good as engaged when Charles was . . . oh around twenty-five. They were living together as well, I think, but that's neither here nor there. Tim, at that time, was abroad for his firm . . . he'd been in Borneo for three years. He came back to London Office, was introduced to Dal and fell for her, hook, line and sinker. Tim was wellplaced at that time; he'd been left a

160

legacy by his god-mother; presumably he dangled this in front of Dal's nose and before you could blink she'd thrown Charles over and was firmly married to Tim.'

'I see.'

'It was tough for Charles, Janina. He'd been anxious to marry Dal . . . he just wanted to wait until he'd got a better position with Rudgleys.'

'I suppose he was . . . very upset.'

'He was, poor lad . . . took him a long time to get over it. He's a fighter, though, takes after me . . . he managed it in the end.'

'Did he?'

'Course he did . . . best day's work he ever did when he got married to you. Unfortunately Dal got her claws into him again.'

'Yes.'

'You noticed, did you?'

'Uncle Joce, I was . . . *am* married to Charles. You can't live with a man, as his wife, for four whole years and not be aware that . . . things have changed.'

'Don't be too hard on Charles. I know him remember, I've seen him grow up. She ran after him, hounded him . . . I dare bet on that . . . probably waylaid him all over the place . . . made his life hell, poor chap.'

'He could have got rid of her if he wanted to. He'd only got to *tell* her!'

'Telling wouldn't deter her. The more he tried to put her off the keener she'd become, particularly if she suspected that he still lusted after her.'

'Well, thank you.'

'My dear girl, you've got to face facts. Men are polygamous by nature, they can fancy more than one, but that needn't affect their marriages . . . oh dear me no. Nevertheless it's something that has to be controlled. Charles, I'm convinced was doing his level best.'

'It must have been very uncomfortable for him.'

He shot me another of his lightning looks. 'This is a serious matter, Janina. And you're wrong to have left Charles . . . wrong and unwise. Even if he'd spent a weekend with the girl, you'd still have been wrong and unkind. Your place is with him. It's always up to the women to ride these little storms . . . they're bound to brew up now and then.'

'I like reasonable calm, and I loathe stormy weather.'

'Then you should never have married a redheaded chap!'

I said no more. I knew it was no use. In the end he went away looking just as baffled as father, but blowing out his cheeks rather more.

★   ★   ★

And then incredibly one morning the tide began to turn. I felt better, optimistic, I woke up noticing things, silly ordinary things like the sun on the wall and the bustle in the street outside.

I ate my breakfast in the kitchen, opening the back door, which looked out on to the garden wall. Beyond the wall was the street . . . I was sand-wiched between streets, for there was one at the front door as well. But the back did have this tiny square of garden just before the wall began.

There was a lot of noise this morning for Tuesday was market day. Traders were busy erecting their stalls, vans were being unloaded, awnings pulled out; carcases of meat looking absolutely grisly were borne along by stalwart men.

It was a far cry from Clayborough, but fun nevertheless. Farther up the hill I could hear the clatter of the trains, especially the goods ones which made the most noise . . . bang . . . bang . . . banga . . . bang . . . banga . . . bang . . . bang.

So washing-up, tidying-up, I took myself in hand. I must stop drifting, I must begin to plan. A job was the thing. I'd have to see about that, I'd register at one of the agencies in the town. I'd aim to start work within the next two weeks, even if it were only part-time. But this morning I'd shop and garden and cook. I hadn't cooked much in the four weeks I'd been here, just lived off salads and cheese. Then straight after lunch I'd go down on the beach and soak up some of the sun.

I thought about lots of things as I weeded and cleared the garden. It was obvious, of course, that Charles and I must divorce. He hadn't been to see me; he didn't want me back; he hadn't even written, or telephoned, or *anything*. If he'd been upset about my leaving home he'd have been down here by now. Father was right; we'd got married too soon: the attraction of opposites, a precarious attraction, a kind of trap, an un-tender trap, for it only led to trouble in the end. I'd known these things, of course, for quite some time; I'd been aware of them deep down in the core of my being; I'd just never dared to take them out and look at them properly in case they were impossible to solve. Dal had done that; she had *made* me see them; she had gouged out the trouble like a glutinous eye and dangled it under my nose. The thought of her and Charles together was too painful to dwell on long . . . it seemed the utmost betrayal . . . it was as if I didn't matter. Perhaps, in a way, I ought to accept it as inevitable because it had started up long 'before me' had never ever burnt itself out. Yet it should have been cancelled out when Charles and I married . . . therefore I had failed in some way . . . There lay the hurt in my own failure to hold him, to make him forget her as though she had never been.

I pulled out an enormous thistle . . . I banged the soil off its roots, then I hoed the garden down flat. There wasn't a thing in it, it was absolutely barren; something would have to be done about that . . . some shrubs perhaps, I could plant them in the autumn, just before Estelle came down.

I went into the house and drank a glass of milk. Of one thing I was certain . . . absolutely certain . . . I would never marry again . . . never, never, ever. I'd be free just as soon as the divorce was through and that was the way I'd stay. I'd be free, I'd be me, I might even change my name . . . I might be Nina Cullimore again.

That afternoon I met Duncan Stevens completely and absolutely by chance.

I'd been swimming and was lying full-length on the beach, when a voice hailed me from a great height.

'Nina . . . it *is* Nina, isn't it?'

There were crowds of people around me, lying jammed like sardines. I sat up carefully, shading my eyes, and there he was looking all legs and trousers, viewed from my position on the sand. I manoeuvred for space and managed to stand. 'Hullo, isn't it crowded and . . . and hot?'

'Yes, I was going to swim, but think I'll give up. You look stunning . . . very brown.'

'Brighton suits me I think.'

We picked our way over layers of bodies and managed to reach the ramp.

'Nina . . . I heard from home about, about you and Charles.'

'Oh yes . . . oh well . . . ' I shrugged, I hoped carelessly and took my sundress out of my bag. It was white like my swimsuit with a broad black belt. I felt stronger covered up as though by buttoning my dress I could hide what I felt inside. Annoyingly in the insipient way chance moods have, my depression was returning full flood.

He kept hold of my beach bag, carrying it for me, as we walked together over the stones.

'Couldn't we have tea together . . . get out of this mob. We could gorge ourselves on cream cakes and forget our woes . . . pretend we're in Brighton on a trip!'

'I'll settle for that.' I answered promptly, and as he smiled back I could see he was surprised that I'd agreed to do as he said.

We crossed the road by the Albion and went up North Street, pushing against another huge tide of people making their way down to Castle Square. Eventually we 'made it' into Western Road, where we sat at a table in an upstairs restaurant and watched another stream of people pass by there.

'Estelle was right about Brighton being 'chocka' in the summer.'

'It's the height of the holiday season now. Nina, you've lost weight. You were reed slim before, now your bones show clearly.'

'I've been told I have excellent bones.' I was determined to be cheerful, but my hands gave me away and my coffee (I detest tea) flopped in my cup.

'You have beautiful bones . . . artistically speaking, but seriously . . . are you making out all right?'

The concern in his eyes nearly finished me for good. Don't sympathise for goodness sake, or I'll bawl like a baby; be bracing and 'don't care' and jolly me along . . . don't look at me as though you see only too clearly the sense of futility that tears me apart.

'Apart from my conscience, I'm over the hump!' The pastry was the sort with candied peel and icing . . . it stuck on my teeth like glue.

'Whatever happened between you I shall never believe that you were the one who . . . well who strayed.'

'There doesn't have to be a guilty party these days . . . but one feels guilt because marriage is meant to be for life . . . you promise that it shall be you see.'

'Anyone can make a mistake.'

'It's a big one to make and difficult to put right.'

'Any chance of your coming together again.'

'No.'

'Want to talk about it?'

'No.'

'You'll have to talk to someone eventually you know, if and when you intend to divorce.'

'We haven't got as far as that . . . but I expect we will. We might have that thing called a judicial separation.'

'Have you discussed the future with your husband?'

'No, not yet.' Pride prevented me from telling him the truth, that I'd had no word from Charles for four whole weeks. I'd have to get in touch with him pretty soon now . . . we couldn't keep drifting like this.

Duncan walked back with me to the cottage afterwards, through the ever crowded, traffic laden streets. Queues were forming at the 'bus stops now as offices and shops disgorged their workers and everyone was rushing to get home.

'I shall have to get a job soon,' I remarked to Duncan, 'although goodness knows what kind.'

'You intend to stay in Brighton?'

'Until the autumn when Estelle comes. After that . . . who knows.'

'All the agencies are advertising temporary jobs. Perhaps you could get one of those.'

'Yes . . . perhaps.'

Conversation lapsed as we neared

Forge Lane, I wondered if I should ask Duncan in. It seemed the obvious thing to do, yet I shrank from actually doing it. I didn't want him to feel he could call there any time. I wanted our relationship to keep very casual . . . a chance wave in the street, an occasional, odd meeting, but nothing of actual design. So I put my key in the lock, turned round on the step and smilingly held out my hand.

'Thank you, I enjoyed that.'

'My pleasure.'

He relinquished my hand, but didn't move off. I backed a little to the door.

'Look, Nina, I know how you feel . . . I know what you're thinking . . . I wouldn't dream of pushing my luck, but . . . well, after all, we are related in a way. If it wouldn't rock the boat too much couldn't we meet sometime . . . have a drink together . . . even a walk wouldn't break the rules too much. There are some wonderful beauty spots all around here, and you've still got that trip to make to

Fawding Head.'

'I know, but . . . '

'I repeat, I'll not push my luck . . . I'll be as remote as you like, but I won't trot out that stupid old adage about just being good friends. Of course you may prefer to be on your own . . . in which case . . . '

'I *did* want to be on my own at first, but now perhaps . . . well yes it would be nice to meet.'

'Good . . . that's better, that's much better, that's great. I'll ring you . . . I know the number, so goodbye until then.'

Touching my shoulder, turning briskly, he made off down the street, turning the corner by the Fox and Dog and the tatty Bed and Breakfast sign.

I went inside feeling thoughtful. I wondered if I'd been wise. Wise or not it was comforting to know that I wasn't completely alone. It was undeniably pleasant to have someone near at hand to turn to if things went wrong. I felt this was weak of me. I ought to be independent, but independence is a seed which has to grow gradually and I'd never had to cultivate it before. Charles had made every decision that was necessary. He'd encouraged, even insisted, that I leaned on him.

Before then I'd leaned on father; I'd never been very 'free-standing'. And the only major decision I'd taken on my own had led to disaster in the end.

But Charles *persuaded* you to marry him . . . what rot he only asked you. You could have said no, you could have played for time, you didn't have to jump recklessly in.

This was how the voices argued in my head . . . telling me off . . . taking me to task.

Look things in the face, Janina Redman. You're always trying to shed the blame.

8

Duncan was right about temporary jobs. There were plenty about and the agency found me one. It was at a boarding school (Foley Hall) on the outskirts of the town. It was a job for the vacation period only, stencilling and filing and bringing records up-to-date. It wasn't very onerous, but I liked it because I could do it. I met people whom I liked and whom I felt liked me. I made friends, I regained confidence, yet I was still in suspense . . . I'd heard absolutely nothing from Charles.

In the end I did what I should have done before. I sat down and wrote to him. I suggested that we met, that I went up to Town, that we discussed the future and made proper plans . . . either to separate legally or divorce: 'I'm sure you will be as glad as me to get something settled. Perhaps you could tell me what you think.'

A week passed and he didn't reply. He must have got the letter because I'd addressed it c/o Rudgleys; I didn't know if he were living at 'High Walls'. Supposing he never replied. What would I do if he refused to see me? I couldn't go on, day after day, drifting along like this. It was seven weeks now since I'd left 'High Walls'. He must have decided on something in his mind.

And then he came, in person, without warning, one evening. I'd just got home from work and was unlocking the door, when I heard footsteps stop at my heels.

'Hullo, Nina.'

'Charles!' I stood and stared at him. I could feel my face paling . . . the back of my neck went stiff. 'Hello, Charles.'

'May I come in?'

'Of . . . of course, please do.' After the initial stab of shock I was fairly calm. My knees shook a bit but that was only to be expected . . . appearing like that and so suddenly too, after so many weeks apart. I banged the door to and took him into the lounge. The little house smelt stuffy, I pushed a sash down. I suggested I should make some tea.

'No, don't bother. I don't think I could drink it.' He seemed just a little unsure of himself. He passed a hand over his face, as though he were tired. 'It's been a long time.' His expression was puzzling, I couldn't read behind it. I was aware of the hammering of my heart.

'Seven weeks exactly. I thought I ought to write. I mean I think we ought to decide . . . '

He caught me up quickly, 'Oh quite, I'm glad you did. I called at lunchtime actually, but you seemed to be out.'

'I was. I have a job. I'm never in till evening.'

'Oh.' He was sitting bolt upright on a Windsor chair. It suited him somehow . . . he was a straight sort of man . . . it wasn't in his nature to be devious or mean.

Somewhere, deep inside me, the ice began to melt. He was my husband . . . he was *still* my husband . . . surely he felt that way too.

'Is your job temporary?'

'Yes.'

The clock ticked fussily, someone clomped past the window, the ice-cream van jangled up the street. Charles looked up, our eyes met, some more ice melted . . . I wanted him to take me in his arms.

'What do you think we ought to do?' My voice came out rough and strained.

'We could . . . have another try. Of course it won't be easy . . . nevertheless it might just work.'

His tone was flat, disinterested, he was forcing himself on. I couldn't hold my own retort back.

'You don't sound very sure.'

'I'm sure we ought to make the . . . I'm sure we ought to try.'

'Why?'

'Because we're married. We ought to stay that way . . . we can't back down.'

'I see . . . I understand . . . and in a way I agree, but I think you could have put it a little more humanely.'

'It's difficult to know *how* to put it. I'm doing the best I can.'

And he was trying of course; he was, I could see that, but he couldn't lie or pretend, he just put the case baldly. Neither did he move, or touch me, or persuade, just sat there looking grim and strained.

I was disappointed, hurt, I was torn in two. I could see he wanted me back for reasons of his own, but he hadn't said he loved me . . . I could see he *didn't* love me . . . he was trying to make the best of a very bad job . . . he didn't want to mess up his life. If only he would say something, add something more, show just the tiniest spark of affection, even look me straight in the eye. The seconds ticked by and I knew that he wouldn't.

He was waiting for me to make the next move; the next move . . . a game of chess . . . you talk about marriage as though it's a game of chess . . . that's what he'd said to Dal. He was applying the very same attitude now . . . he wanted to stay married because it was 'done' . . . whatever he might feel inside. And there would always be Dal . . . there would always be Dal. I could see her lying hot and rumpled on the couch, inviting Charles to make love to *her*. The thought of her was agony . . . I'd never live it down . . . I'd never get rid of the pain. And like everything else adultery's just a word . . . it doesn't mean much until it moves in close and applies to the man one loves.

'We can't start living together, Charles. However hard we tried it would simply never work.' I actually sounded brisk. I was harder than I thought.

He jerked in his chair. He even looked surprised. What a cheek he had to look surprised.

'Now look Nina, I can't eat humble pie for the rest of my life . . . all I can promise you here and now is that things will be different. I'll do my best to make you happy. I'll fulfil my part of the bargain all through.'

'*Bargain*!'

'Well ... yes ... marriage is a bargain of a kind.'

'A pledge perhaps ... but a bargain never ... you make it sound like something out of a sale!'

'Do you believe that I mean what I say?'

'I believe *you* believe it.' I felt flat and desperate ... racked with memories too. Sitting there looking at Charles I was reminded of many things ... of Charles cutting the lawn in old denims and shirt, Charles sleek at parties, saying all the right things, of Charles at breakfast, Charles at supper, Charles coming up the drive at night. There were other memories too, private ones, special ones ... wrecked by the two of us hopelessly in discord, wrecked by the shadow of Dal.

'It's no good, we're incompatible!' I managed at last ... 'We don't fit as people, we never agree, we can't even agree to part.'

'If you cared for me at all we could overcome all that.'

He started to move towards me, but I jumped to my feet. It was too late now to try loving measures, simply as a means to an end . . . it was wrong to switch them on like a sort of handy gadget . . . they had to come naturally from deep inside.

'No, Charles . . . no! I couldn't live as we did!'

'If you come back with me now you can do exactly as you like.'

'You can't make terms . . . you can't *do* that! Our marriage was a mistake . . . I think we should admit it. I think we should cut free now.'

'I do love you, you know.'

This was so unconvincing, so untrue, that it was all I could do not to laugh. He hadn't even bothered to make it *sound* true; it was as if he'd slipped the words into his mouth like sweets, especially to slide them out again.

'Perhaps you do,' I said carefully, 'perhaps you do in your way.'

'Well, for crying out loud, what other way is there . . . I can't love you in anyone else's way! Perhaps that's it . . . perhaps that's at the root of it . . . perhaps you've found someone down here who loves you in *his* way! Is that the case, Janina . . . is that it . . . is that it . . . is that what it's all about!'

He crossed the room and glared at me, his face an inch from mine. 'Now listen to me . . . I'm not going down on my bended knees, but I'm nevertheless asking you, asking you in all . . . sincerity . . . to come back to me, to come back home, and start living a decent life again!'

'No.'

'What!' He grabbed me, then released me, and I reeled against a chair. I felt it skid over the floor.

'You can't bear to be refused anything, can you, Charles . . . you think you can demand all you want!'

'I'll not agree to a divorce . . . you

183

can close your mind to that . . . I'll not divorce, under any circumstances . . . I've seen enough of that to put me off for life!'

'Under the consent thing you have no option.'

'Oh yes I have. *Both* parties have to consent . . . remember . . . unless you're willing to wait five years. And I'm not admitting to the breakdown of *my* marriage, either for you or anyone else!'

'I shall petition for divorce,' I said, my voice shaking wildly, 'on the grounds that *our* marriage has broken down because of your adultery with Dal!'

'You'll *what?*'

'I shall go up to Northumberland and . . . and secure evidence. You shan't keep me tied to you against my will.'

'You'd stoop to that . . . you'd do that to me?'

'If I had to . . . yes.'

Again he stepped close, but I held my ground. I'd never seen him so angry in my life.

'So it's come to that has it? And you're the girl who stood beside me in church, promising to stay with me for the rest of her life . . . till death do us part . . . or don't you remember?'

'I remember . . . oh I remember all right! I also remember that you promised it too, and you've broken the most important vow of all . . . you haven't loved me, properly loved me for months and months and months; you've just yanked me along, or pushed me around, made me conform to you. I haven't felt cherished since we lived over Mr. Fenner's, and on top of all that . . . on top of all that you've co . . . cohabited with someone else!'

He strode away from me, turned his back. I could see his clenched fists, his shoulders were hunched. 'All right . . . you win . . . let's split and have done with it, and you needn't bother with your snooping up in Northumberland; we'll separate properly, for two more years and have a clean divorce on those grounds. I'll pay the fees, of course.'

'We'll pay half each. I can easily afford it. It'll be the last thing we'll share!'

The look on his face nearly finished me for good . . . he couldn't really hate me quite as much as that. 'You've changed, Janina.'

'One changes according to circumstances and circumstances have changed.'

'I never dreamt you could be like this.'

'Well I can . . . quite easily . . . it's a good thing you've found me out. What a good thing we've made this *mutual* discovery . . . that we're each of us nasty in separate ways. Now the rest of our lives needn't be blighted by one another . . . we can each of us grow up straight.'

We walked in silence along the passage to the narrow front door. He turned round with his hand on the catch.

'You'd better collect what belongs to

you from 'High Walls' some time. So far as I'm concerned you can take what you like . . . it doesn't mean much to me now.'

'I'll fetch my clothes when you're not there. I still have my key.'

'I'm not there at all. I'm living in Town. If you need to get in touch with me use the office number. I suppose now I'll have to tell the news to father. I've kept quiet about it so far.'

'He'll be upset, but he'll get over it.'

'He's old, he's feeble, he'll take it very badly. I suppose I've only myself to blame for this.'

The gloom in the hall lent a spurious closeness. I felt a frantic urge to help.

'Charles it's not the fault of either of us . . . it's both of us together. We made a mistake . . . it's unfortunate, terrible, but it isn't a crime; neither is divorce, not now, not these days; in a way it's . . . commonplace.'

'It's failure in block letters, three feet high. It's soul-destroying too, the ultimate in let-downs!'

'But, Charles . . . '
'Goodbye, Janina.'
He stepped into the street and pulled the door to; it closed with a gentle snap.

9

'I'd like to go back to my maiden name.'

'You could call yourself Cullimore, if you liked.' Duncan drained his glass, set it down on the table. It was Sunday and we were in a bar on the Front, having a pre-lunch drink. Duncan had rung me up shortly after Charles had been down. I'd been rather glad to go out.

'Could I?'

'Why yes, there's no law against anyone calling themselves anything, so long as they don't go signing cheques, or documents in a fictitious name.'

'And I could leave off my rings?'

He looked faintly surprised and I felt an instant's shame. 'Yes, if you wanted to.'

'I do want to . . . I do want to!' Yet as I twisted the rings round, tugged them off, looked at my hand lying bare on the table, I felt a steady anguish which I couldn't sustain. I swiftly put them on again.

'Nina . . . ' He covered my hand with his, 'take it easy, darling. You're rushing things . . . it's early days yet . . . try and take it piece by piece. You're unhappy and restive, but you won't always be. Things will improve with time.'

'Whilst I'm married to Charles I must wear his rings.'

'Of course you must, if you feel that way.'

'And use his name.'

'That too.'

'I expect you think I'm potty.'

'I think you still care for him . . . more than you realise.'

That was it, of course, he'd hit the nail on the head; he was a very intuitive man. I looked at him and smiled. I liked him so much. In the two months I'd been living here I'd met him four times; once by accident, three times by arrangement. But up until now, up until this morning, I really hadn't minded whether I did so or not. Looking at him now I couldn't be quite so flip, I knew that I liked him a lot. It was because of the total break with Charles, of course; Nature abhorring a vacuum was filling mine up fast . . . or doing her level best.

'We were happy at first,' I explained more calmly, 'and there were many times afterwards when it was very, very good. If it had been *all* unhappiness there'd be no problem . . . now the parts that were happy keep coming back to mind, like the good points of someone who's died. And I'm lonelier and more . . . more desperate since Charles came.'

'Did he want you to go back to him?'

'Yes.'

'Why didn't you?'

'I can't explain exactly,' I sipped a second gin and tonic which I didn't really want. Gin made me maudlin at the best of times; there was no need to accentuate my mood, 'I don't know why. I just couldn't, that's all. You see he never really wanted me exactly as I was. Charles always hoped that I'd change.'

'You mean he hoped to change you.'

'I suppose so.'

Duncan looked reflective. 'A new angle that . . . it's usually the woman who tries to change the man . . . or so I'm told.'

'Yes.' I *was* tight, I could feel my arms going rubbery. I decided to leave the rest of my drink.

'Anyway you don't need changing . . . you're perfect as you are . . . beautiful, loyal and sweet.'

'Not very loyal, talking like this.' But I smiled because the compliments had pleased me no end . . . lovely to be approved of like this. And having started smiling I found I couldn't stop. I went on like the Cheshire cat.

'Oh, Nina! If only . . . if only . . . ' Duncan lifted my hand, pressed it to his cheek, then held it enclosed in his. I let it lie there, all tingly and delicious whilst his fingers curled tightly round mine. 'Just supposing,' he went on, 'you had been unattached, when we met at our respective parents' wedding reception . . . would you have liked me at all?'

'I expect so. It's . . . very difficult to tell.'

'Oh.' He made a small face at me and released my hand. I could have told him I liked him now, that I'd just discovered how much, but I didn't because it might have been a distortion of the truth. It might have been the gin, or the state I was in . . . off with the old, on with the new . . . we all know the danger of that.

So I was glad when he reverted to his normal casual self, as we walked along the promenade and on to the pier for a breath of sea air before lunch. Duncan was easy to be with; one didn't *have* to talk. Any silences between us were friendly and unfraught. There was a placidity about him that made oneself unwind, like sitting in a nice green field.

'Just think,' he said, as the sea thundered beneath us, glimpsed now and then through the stout wooden slats, 'just supposing we'd married, become husband and wife, think how neat and tidy it would all have been; my father-in-law would have been my step-father as well . . . '

'And Valerie my mother-in-law! A bit too neat and pat really, don't you think? Real life doesn't work out that way!'

We were at the end of the pier now; there were fewer people here . . . only a fisherman or two. The fishermen reminded me of the river at Clayborough. Estelle had liked Duncan . . . but how could she be off it . . . he was a very attractive man. Yet the air blew differently from the way it did at Clayborough, and the sea was a clear shade of turquoise-blue with indigo streaks like puddles of ink when the clouds passed over the sun. We stood on the port-side and looked towards the shore . . . there was the faintest of mists inland.

I caught my breath; for a second I was transported. 'Isn't it beautiful, Duncan

. . . isn't it absolutely lovely . . . '

'*You* are lovely, absolutely lovely . . . you must know how lovely you are.'

He put his hand on the back of my neck under my hair and kissed me full on the mouth. The entrancement was complete and I couldn't speak at all as I rested against his cheek. When he released me I swayed against the rail. His arm supported me, we walked back to the turnstile. We both of us knew our relationship had changed, that it couldn't be changed back again.

The bustle of the town brought us back to earth again. We toiled up the hill to Estelle's house.

'Who's going to grill those succulent steaks?' Duncan had brought enough food that morning to feed a family of six.

'You can,' I told him, 'I'll be lazy . . . the gin's gone straight to my head!'

'Nina . . . '

'Yes?'

'You're a wonderful girl!'

'And you are a wonderful booster of egos!'

He took the key from me and unlocked the front door, and as we went inside, shut it behind us, as we stood in the gloom of the narrow little hall, I was so swept with feeling, so keyed for his touch, I felt that I'd die if he left me alone. It was the gin, of course, I was drunk, I was tipsy, but I didn't care, I didn't care, I just didn't care . . . if he didn't make love to me I'd die on the spot . . . I'd drop down dead where I stood.

'Janina . . . Janina . . . my darling girl!'

I was in his arms, tight in his arms . . . I'd forgotten how warm a man's body was . . . I'd forgotten . . . I'd forgotten . . . or perhaps I remembered . . . the pressure . . . the warmth . . . the jarring weakness . . . the roaring tide of energy within. 'Janina . . . Janina . . . '

Then back to earth . . . separation . . . the shrilling of a bell.

'Your 'phone . . . '

'I'll answer it.'

'Leave it . . . '

'No, I can't . . . '

But in the end it was he who lifted the receiver. And I went into the lounge.

I sank down on the couch, my legs stiff as boards, tears poured down my cheeks on to the backs of my hands. I looked at them foolishly, I must be crying, I didn't seem able to stop. Then Duncan again, looking strangely unfamiliar, his face wearing an odd sort of look.

'It's a Mr. Jocelyn Redman. Someone has died.'

'Oh no, Duncan! *No!*'

I suppose I must have got to the telephone somehow, for there was Uncle Joce's voice bellowing in my ear.

'It's bad news Janina, very bad news. Tim's been killed in a car crash in Toronto.'

'You did say . . . Tim?' It was awful to feel relief, but just for a second I did.

'Afraid so, poor boy, he was killed

outright. He wasn't driving, he was the passenger in the car . . . some sort of pile-up, I understand.'

'I'm dreadfully sorry Uncle Joce . . . I don't know what else to say.'

'He's being flown home . . . funeral's on Friday . . . in the family plot, interment, of course.'

'Dal?' I could hardly say her name, even then.

'Taken it badly, very shocked.'

'And . . . and Charles?'

'Very upset. Now look, Janina, I want you to come to the funeral.'

'Come to the . . . but Uncle Joce, I don't think Charles would want that, I don't think he'd want me to.'

'I haven't discussed it with Charles.'

'But I couldn't come unless he said so . . . unless he wanted me there.'

'Don't raise difficulties where none exist. You should be here, you're part of the family, one of the Redmans, whether you like it or not!'

'But Charles wouldn't expect, wouldn't want me to come. There'd be . . . it'd

cause embarrassment . . . you don't understand.'

'I don't care a tit or tattle about any
silly embarrassment . . . I'm concerned
for my brother, that's all.'

'For Sir William, but . . . '

'Tim was Will's favourite son. He's
over eighty and he's frail, this could be
the death of him . . . *will* be if he
thinks there's trouble between you and
Charles. The family means a great deal
to him, a very great deal. He'll notice if
you're not there, he'll look out for you,
query your absence. He's fond of you
. . . we all are . . . don't let us down
over this.'

I swallowed hard, my head spun with
doubt. Out of the corner of my eye I
saw Duncan's green shirt as he moved
across the hall. From the receiver came
the stertorous sound of Uncle Joce's
breathing; from the *way* he breathed I
could tell he was het up, yet the thought
of doing what he asked unnerved me.
Dal would be there, she'd most likely
be with Charles; I'd have to join them

to make it look right. It'd create an absolutely awful contretemps. I'd feel like some sort of ghastly avenging angel . . . I'd be the very last person they'd want.

I shifted the receiver, speaking directly into its 'mouth'.

'I can't decide spot on, not right away, Uncle Joce. I'll think about it this afternoon and ring you back. I'll ring you just before six.'

'All right, my dear. I'll await your call.' He was very pleasant about it; he didn't attempt to press, and that fact surprised me most of all.

Duncan's face was grave when I told him the news.

'What a terrible thing. What sort of age was he?'

'Thirty-five . . . three years older than Charles.' And I was silent as I remembered the last time I'd seen Tim, sulking in the garden after his quarrel with Charles . . . zipping down our drive in the little red car, after a perfunctory goodbye. Awful for Charles not to see him again . . . awful to have parted like that.

'Were they fond of each other, the two brothers?'

'Oh yes . . . oh I don't know . . . I suppose so. Duncan, Uncle Joce wants me to go to the funeral. It's on Friday, from Horley Wood . . . my father-in-law's home.'

'Will you go? Is it something you feel you ought to do?'

'I don't want to, but yes I feel I ought.'

'It's really . . . entirely up to you.'

'And I ought to write to Tim's wife. I ought to write to Dal. In spite of what happened I ought to rise above it . . . I oughtn't to let it matter now.'

'I'm not quite with you, Nina. What is it that shouldn't matter?'

I looked at Duncan feeling helpless. I didn't know what to do. Once again I was so used to Charles ordering my days, I couldn't be clear cut on my own.

'Dal is . . . was Tim's wife. She was

one of the reasons why I left Charles. She and he were . . . are . . . they love one another.'

'I *see.*'

He joined me on the couch, picking up my hands, kissing the palms one by one. 'You've never told me this before.'

'I couldn't.'

'I just thought you and Charles didn't hit it off. I didn't know there was . . . another girl.'

'Dal was always Charles' girl.' And then holding his hands I told him the rest of the tale.

'But Nina . . . but darling . . . in these circumstances, do you really think any good will come of your going to the funeral? It seems to me it could make for still more unhappiness, especially as Tim's wife will be there.'

'That's what I thought, but Uncle Joce said . . . '

'Nina . . . don't go!' He was suddenly urgent . . . his eyes locked with mine . . . 'don't go, don't get involved! I know how you feel, you are still one of the family, but it's a tricky situation, very tricky indeed. It could be awkward, you might get hurt.'

'Charles may want me there.'

'In view of what you've told me, I doubt that very much.'

'Duncan!'

'Well I'm sorry, but put yourself in his place . . . consider how he feels. Guilty as hell, loathing the sight of himself, unable to make his peace with his brother . . . hating Dallas, hating you, but most of all hating himself. And you are the one who knows all this . . . he knows you know it . . . and he'll hate you for that knowledge. He'll rather you kept away.'

'I may be able to help him.'

'It would be unwise of you to try.'

'He's my husband. I know him better than you do!'

'I'm a man. I know my sex; they don't like feeling guilty. They're apt to lash out when they do!'

We cooked and ate our lunch which we neither of us enjoyed, and pretty soon afterwards Duncan left. I knew there was sense in what he advised, but at six o'clock that evening when I rang Uncle Joce it was to tell him that I'd be at the funeral on Friday.

It was to give a definite 'yes'.

10

I got a stopping train to Horley Wood and a taxi to The Lodge, where the funeral cortege would begin.

The drive was jammed with cars, the hall banked with flowers; I pushed around through crowds of people desperately looking for Charles. The purpose of my coming was to make a pair with Charles; that was the whole idea. I found him in the library, talking to the housekeeper; of Dallas there was no sign.

I was shocked at Charles' appearance. His face was putty white and drawn. He smiled like a tired old man.

'Good of you to come, Nina . . . thanks.'

'I'm very sorry about it Charles; you know that, don't you?'

'You'd better have a word with father. He doesn't know we're living apart.'

'It's all right ... I know that ... Uncle Joce explained.'

If anything Charles looked worse than Sir William. The old man, long-whiskered, like an ancient seal, was a model of composure compared with his son.

'A bad business, Janina ... a very bad business. You must take care of Charles, he's all I've got now. The boy had the sense to pick a good wife ... not so easy to find these days.'

'Sir William ... ' I bent to kiss him, his cheek smelt of pepper, or I suppose it could have been snuff.

'Can't make out why Dallas isn't here?' He looked at me as if I ought to know.

'She's ill, father, I told you.' Charles' voice came sharply over the top of my head. The old man grimaced and reached for my arm, as he hauled himself to his feet.

'We're all ill at times like this ... ill, sick at heart, sick of life maybe.'

It was terrible of me, I know, but I

could only feel relief that I wouldn't have to meet Dal after all. I wouldn't have to see her and Charles together; there was a limit to what I could stand.

'I'm sorry Dal's ill.' I said to Charles, as we waited for the cars to line up.

'Are you?'

'Well of course I am. It must be dreadful for her.'

'It's dreadful for us all, God knows.'

All through the church service and the short one at the graveside, Charles stood beside me, stiff as a board, careful not to touch me, or even bend my way. I could feel his distress as though it were my own, but as we turned away and I touched his arm, he made a little movement as though to shake me off and my hand fell back to my side.

Our car returned far more swiftly than it'd come, slipping silently under the avenue of trees that led away from the cemetery gates. The sun was shining and the trees made shadows which flowed over the bonnet like rivulets of rain. On the open road it was hot and airless; Charles opened a window on his side. But he didn't speak to me and my throat constricted; surely there was something he could say.

Back at The Lodge I handed round refreshments to the crowd of relatives and friends. Uncle Joce and Sir William sat stoically side-by-side. I caught Uncle Joce's eye on me once or twice and I knew that once again he was trying to play God; once again he was convinced that he knew best, and that flinging Charles and me together, even at a funeral, would ward off a final split.

Afterwards, still for appearances' sake, I left with Charles in his car. I thought he intended to take me to the station, but as we drove along he suggested I came to 'High Walls' and packed up some of my things.

'All right.' (Silly to feel he was pushing me out . . . stupid to feel like that.)

'If you feel like it, of course.'

'I think it's a good idea.'

'I'll get that cabin trunk out of the

back of the garage. If you put everything in there I'll see it's sent direct . . . direct to Estelle's house.'

'Thank you.'

Perhaps something in my voice got past his guard, for he glanced at me briefly and said.

'It's not a case of a clean sweep, Nina, but you see I'm selling the house.'

'*Selling* it . . . selling 'High Walls'?'

'Seems best, don't you think, in all the circumstances. Prices are high now, might as well take advantage. I'll send you half the proceeds, of course.'

'Half the proceeds! But whatever for? I don't want that!' I was appalled at the suggestion; it was like compensation, like paying me off, like paying me something to get out, 'I don't want that; the house is in your name. It's yours and only yours; it doesn't belong to me!'

'It was given to me by father because of our marriage. Morally, if not legally, half of it's yours.' He was using a well-remembered tone of voice — conciliatory, tolerant, talking 'down', as one would to a backward child. But I didn't say anything because I didn't want to quarrel, and anyway even if he sent me the money I could always, later on, send it back.

We reached 'High Walls', we walked up the drive. The house looked familiar, yet strange-faced too, as though it were wearing an expression I didn't know on purpose to put me off. Its inside smelt different as we entered the hall. It could have belonged to someone else already; it could have already been sold.

'It doesn't feel like our home any more.'

'Well it's not, so I suppose that's the reason why.'

There were roses in a bowl on the telephone table. I buried my nose in them, hiding my face, but they scarcely had any scent at all.

'Everywhere looks . . . very clean.'

'Mrs. Dean come in every other day. If you'd like to go up and collect your things, I'll get the cabin trunk in from the garage, and help you carry them down.'

'Thank you.' I said and went towards the stairs, climbing them with legs that were none too steady, clinging to the banister rail. When I reached the landing Charles was still in the hall, staring up at me as though I were a ghost. I looked towards the bedroom feeling hesitant and gauche. 'Charles, is it all right to . . . '

'Don't be silly.'

So I took a deep breath and stepped inside, but I needn't have worried — there was nothing to remind me of past intimacies. The entire room had an unlived-in look, only the furniture was the same and the carpet and the curtains. The dressing table mirror seemed to reflect a different girl . . . a large-eyed thin one in a dark green dress, with a wide-brimmed dark green hat. The hat didn't suit me, it made me look macabre; I took it off and laid it on the bed. The bed wasn't made up and there were none of Charles' things about. I didn't know what that meant, except that he'd moved out; perhaps he was living in Town with Dal.

So only my own clothes hung in the big double wardrobe. I scooped them out in armfuls, hangers as well, and dumbled them down in the hall. The whole operation took only a quarter of an hour; I was done long before Charles came in from the garage, pulling the cabin trunk along on trolley wheels, opening it up and dusting it and lining it with paper, then leaving me to pack it on my own.

'When you've finished we'll have a sherry, then I'll run you to the station. I'll label the trunk when you've gone.' He went into the lounge and closed the door behind him. I supposed he wanted to be on his own.

My own feelings were completely null and void. I felt numb, anaesthetised, not like me at all. This was someone else's hall I was kneeling and packing in; there was nothing in it to bring back a single nostalgic pang; even the bowl that held the roses didn't belong to me; it must be one brought in by Mrs. Dean. How could things change so much in only nine weeks; it seemed more like nine years.

Yet nervousness speared through the numbness in my brain as I packed the last few garments, swung the lid back into place, pressed down the stiff metal hasps. I was going into the lounge to have a drink with Charles. This would be the last time I'd meet him face to face, except when we went to Court in two years' time, admitting to the public and the world in general that yet another marriage had broken down.

So far had we drifted in the past nine weeks that I felt I ought to tap at the door before I entered . . . but how absurd, how absurd when it was partly my house, when we were still, at this day, husband and wife. So I managed not to tap, but I opened the door quietly, standing with the knob still turned in my hand, staring over the carpet at Charles.

He was sitting in the armchair that used to be mine. There were two glasses of sherry on the table beside him. His elbows were on his knees, his face in his hands. As his hands drew down and I saw the misery in his eyes, everything I ever felt for him rose full flood I rushed across the room to his side.

'Charles . . .'

For a second he seemed to hesitate, then pushed me away. He thrust a glass of sherry at me, jerked out a chair. 'Allow me a bit of latitude for God's sake . . . Tim *was* my brother you know!'

'Well of *course* he was . . . I *know* that . . . that's what I *mean*! Charles I want to help . . . I want to help so much! I want to be *with* you in this!'

He gave me a long, steady, hard-faced look. I felt I'd dreamed the other one up. 'Let's keep a sense of proportion shall we? No point in making a gesture grande dame, when it's already too late.'

'I don't know what you mean!'

'If you don't know, I can't tell you.'

'All I know is I want to help . . . I want to stay with you and help!'

'You can't help, you never could!'

'Charles!'

'So drink up and let's be off . . . no point in prolonging things more than we need.'

All the way to the station, all the way to Brighton in the semi-fast train, the curt words jolted and jarred through my head in a constant repetitive refrain . . . you can't help, you never could, you can't help you never could.

I felt they'd bang through my head for ever. I felt I'd never get them out.

It was dark when the train eased into Brighton station, dark and raining, much cooler too. I felt stiff and cold and prickly as I crossed the station yard. I didn't think I could manage even the short walk home. I hailed a taxi and climbed inside.

The road was wet and shiny, a mirror for the lights. The whole street was full of glare and glitter and noise. I wished I were already in bed. And then we were turning left down the hill, left again along Forge Lane.

'What number, madam?'

'Twenty-three . . . the one next to 'The Fox and Dog'.' There were a lot of people milling in and out of the pub. I could smell the beer, hear the juke box, hear the bar-man laugh. And then as I got out of the cab on to the pavement, I noticed something else.

There was a light on in my lounge and in the bedroom above. There were two rectangles of light.

I stood and stared at them, feeling rather dazed, whilst the rain pelted down on my hat.

'That'll be 25p if you don't mind, madam.'

'Oh yes, of course, I'm sorry. Here you are.'

I was foraging in my bag when the front door opened and there silhouetted like a picture in a frame was a tall slim figure in a hostess gown, her hair in a thick black braid.

'Estelle . . . Good Lord . . . what a fright you gave me!'

Her sleeves were long and full like wings; she reached out and pulled me inside. 'Thank goodness, I was getting worried . . . my angel, you're soaking wet!'

'But, Estelle, why ever didn't you tell me you were coming,' and then I stopped, remembering just in time that this was her home and she had a perfect right to come and go as she pleased.

'I meant to and then I didn't think it mattered. I'm a whole month earlier than I intended, but Willow Barn's being re-roofed, so I thought I'd clear out. But my dear girl you look absolutely done to death . . . go and get dry; I'll heat something up.'

'I've been . . . '

'I know where you've been, Duncan rang an hour ago, expecting to speak to you. He told me all about it.'

'Oh.'

'Oh yes . . . and a man called . . . a funny little man, small and fair and wispy, rather nondescript. He asked for Miss Cullimore, or rather if Miss Cullimore lived here. Are you using your maiden name, by the way?'

'No, I'm *not*! Who was it? What did he want?'

'My sweet, I haven't the faintest. After I said you lived here he sort of slunk away. The funny thing is . . . the odd thing was I seem to remember meeting him before.'

'I don't suppose . . . ' I said tiredly, 'it was anything very much.' I dragged myself heavily up the stairs.

As I changed into slacks and sweater, brushed out my hair, I wondered what on earth I'd better do. As Estelle was back I'd have to move out, at least in a day or two.

But when I put this to her she vetoed it at once.

'What nonsense, there are two bedrooms, room for us both. I do have . . . certain plans, although I can't tell you now, but at any rate you needn't move out.'

'Well, if you're sure.' I began to feel more cheerful, drank a cup of soup; it was nice to be cosseted like this.

'Sure I'm sure,' Estelle was drinking vodka, 'now tell me about today. Who was there? Was it frightful? And why did you have to go?'

I told her as much as I felt she ought to know. She listened in a rapt and thoughtful way, saying nothing for a very long time. Then she came out with something so unspeakable, it was all I could do not to scream.

'Pity . . . in some ways . . . it hadn't been Charles.'

'Estelle! How can you *say* that . . . think it! It's a horrible thing to say!'

'I was thinking of you. It would leave you free at once . . . free to begin again!'

'It's a terrible thing to say!' And then I was silent. I retreated into my skin, for I recognised the look on Estelle's face. She was acting true to form, as a means to an end. She had this habit sometimes when she was fishing for information.

She hacked it out, chopped it out, took a hatchet to it. And then when she'd finished she'd sit back and browse on what she'd contrived to expose. This, I supposed, was the writer in her. Nothing really mattered but her art.

'I didn't mean to upset you.'

'You haven't,' I was determined to be lofty; I went on in the same vein, 'I mean if you're going to kill off whom you please, you might as well say it should have been Dal, then Tim could have got himself a brand new wife and Charles could have come back to me.'

'Would you have him back?'

'No, I would *not*!'

'Ah-ha, so our little Nina hasn't lost her spunk!'

'Or you could . . . ' I persisted, 'say it should have been me, me *as well as* Tim. Then Charles and Dal would both have been free to do whatever they liked.'

'All right . . . all right . . . don't shoot me down! I'm sorry I got carried away.'

'It doesn't matter, Estelle, it doesn't

matter at all. And whichever way you look at it, however terrible it is, Tim's death *will* make things simpler for Charles, when he gets over it, I mean.'

'Simpler, more difficult or quite impossible . . . depending on his nature my lamb.'

'I don't know what you mean.'

'Well Tim's death could cause such a . . . such an eruption in Charles' mind that it could put him off Dallas for life. It could make him hate her and hate himself. Quite probably at this moment he even hates you . . . hates the whole rotten world.'

'He did say . . . did act . . . rather strangely.'

'I'm not surprised. And quite honestly, Nina, if he *does* still keep with Dal, then all I can say is he's a very tough cookie indeed!'

'I felt sorry for him, Estelle.'

'I dare say you did, but for goodness sake keep that sort of feeling within bounds. Don't go rushing back to him on a wave of compassion . . . *that's* not what he needs by a very long chalk. And it wouldn't solve the problem at all!'

I was silent again. I wasn't going to tell her that I'd already 'rushed back', or attempted to do so, and had been pushed away good and hard.

That night I dreamed the funeral all over again . . . the coffin being lowered into the Redman plot . . . the rattling chains . . . the thudding earth . . . the gathered people, the white faces, the flowers, the wreaths, the reek of evergreen . . . and far off . . . somewhere far, far off . . . my own voice shouting on a thread of sound . . . 'no, no, you can't, you can't bury me here . . . I'm not a Redman any more'.

11

Any re-surge of feeling I might have had for Charles was considerably diminished when I began to suspect that he was having me tailed. It was difficult to believe, it was so unlike him, to go back on anything he said.

He'd told me quite definitely that we'd live apart for two years and then get divorced by consent. It now seemed that he just couldn't wait for this; he wanted to divorce *me*, put the onus me, make me the cause of it it all.

Perhaps he really thought I was playing fast and loose. I remembered his words when he'd come down to see me. 'Perhaps you've found someone else down here'. So perhaps he thought I was having an affair.

It didn't make it better that it could have been true. I was attracted to Duncan, I knew he was to me. It was a classic situation, an explosive one too. It could happen easily between Duncan and me. But to be spied on, watched, was the very last straw. And how long had it been going on? I rather thought from about the time I'd gone to Horley Wood . . . from about the time of the funeral a fortnight ago.

And there was another thing too that was extremely odd . . . the little man who skittered behind me in supermarkets and stores, who trailed me to work most days . . . tallied in description to the one who'd called on Estelle, asking for 'Miss Cullimore' at the door.

Duncan treated the whole thing with his usual calm.

'It seems very unlikely he's a 'tail', I think. I don't know much about divorce law, but I thought that private-eye technique was all unnecessary now. I shouldn't think this little man has anything to do with Charles. What's he look like, by the way?'

'Wispy, weedy, about my height, mousy hair set in ridges and he has a funny walk . . . he seems to sort of slither along.'

'Sounds charming, also harmless. Still, you never know. I suppose he's some sort of crank.'

'Well, he knows my maiden name, whoever he is.'

'Yes, your aunt told me . . . puzzling that. But it seems to bear out my thought that he's not employed by Charles. If he were he'd have asked for you as Mrs. Redman, or merely watched and not asked at all.'

'Yes, I know.'

'Could it have been someone you knew when you were single and living at Fawding . . . I mean as he's down this way?'

'I was only seventeen when we left Fawding, and I hardly knew anyone other than schoolfriends, and he's years and years older than me. Oh I'll forget it . . . it's beginning to get a bore. If I see him again I'll ask him outright what he thinks he's at . . . if I can catch him that is. He goes away like a flash as soon as I turn my head.'

Duncan laughed and took my arm. It was Saturday and we were having our usual country hike. 'He sounds more like a scared bunny than a sleuth I must say . . . makes me wonder who's chasing who!'

'Well I'm not chasing him and that's for sure . . . he's not my type at all!'

We laughed together easily. We were used to each other now. And since our impassioned embrace of a few weeks back, we'd both of us put on an intentional brake, keeping our emotions in check.

All in all things weren't going along too badly. Estelle and I got along well at the cottage; the school kept me on after the holidays ended, and I usually met Duncan on Wednesdays and at week-ends, when we walked and talked about all and everything, yet kept off future plans.

But I dreaded the nights. From midnight until dawn I seemed to plumb the depths. Sometimes I slept, of course, but more often I did not, and I'd toss and turn, or get up and walk about, longing for the night to end. Would I ever get used to sleeping alone? Would I ever get used to being single again? How long could I endure this ache of mind and body ... this desolation of being quite alone. Perhaps it would be better after the first whole year. Perhaps I'd grow a thick crustacean shell.

And then there was the dream. I'd had it once or twice ... the dream which in the morning seemed ridiculously funny, but which waking from in the small hours was hideous in the extreme, making me sweat and tremble, feel cold stark fear, which I'd never had to grapple with before. And it was always the same dream ... it never varied at all. It was always exactly the same.

I'd be walking along in lush green countryside. The grass was longish and slightly damp, a fine drizzle was falling all around. It was more of a mist than a drizzle really; the sort that put a veil over trees and sky, clung to my lashes and brows and hair, making it difficult to see. I had on a yellow mackintosh, the stiff shiny sort, belted in at the waist. I kept tramping happily and wetly along, and then I stumbled on a recumbent shape . . . it was a girl, a woman in a mackintosh like mine, lying face down in the grass. She had slender legs, one shoe was off, her hair was dark and long. She lay absolutely still, not moving, not breathing; then as I bent down and pushed to turn her over, she rolled face upwards, eyes staring at the sky. And it was then that the freeze started in my own body, for the face was mine, the glazed eyes were mine, the girl in the mackintosh was me.

I didn't tell Estelle. She might have put it in a script, but I did tell Duncan one day. He said it was all due to being betwixt and between, and that once I was inured to managing without Charles, my nightmares would simmer down; or at least that's what he said at first. And then one Wednesday when we were coming back from Rottingdean where we'd been walking on the ridge by the Mill on Beacon Hill, he said something that set me wondering again.

'Have you still got this so-called sleuth following you around?'

'I've seen him once or twice . . . perhaps not quite so much.'

'I think it might be a good idea to write to your husband, Nina. Ask him if he's set someone on our . . . on your trail. And if he hasn't and the man persists, I'll get in touch with the police.'

'Duncan!'

'I'd rather be on the safe side . . . it's three weeks now . . . and there are some very odd folks around. I don't suppose it's anything . . . anything at all, but we'd better make absolutely sure.'

So because I nearly always do what other people say, I wrote a carefully worded letter to Charles. I found it very difficult and the end result was stilted, but at least it was clear and to the point.

23 Forge Lane,
Brighton, Sussex.
30th September

Dear Charles,

The trunk with all my clothes in arrived the other week. Thank you for putting my mackintosh in. I'd quite forgotten that.

I hope you are feeling better and that things are going well for you. I hope, too, that you have told father-in-law all about us. I can't until you do, and I would like to write to him.

With regard to our divorce, I don't suppose it's necessary for either of us to see a solicitor until we have done the two year living apart bit, but are you by any chance having me watched because there has been a man watching me, and watching the house, on and off since I last saw you, when I came to Horley Wood? If he is employed by you, could you please give him notice, because it's a waste of money for you and very nasty for me. If I were having an affair I'd tell you so because I don't cheat. So perhaps you could do something about the man, please. If I don't hear from you I shall assume you've done it. But if he's nothing to do with you and you don't know what I'm talking about, could you let me know as my step-brother may be calling in the police.

Yours, Nina.

A whole week passed and Charles didn't reply. And it may have been coincidence, or it may not . . . but the little man disappeared.

★　★　★

Duncan and I walked over Fawding Head during the second week in October, on a brilliantly sunny Saturday afternoon. Duncan had got Leila staying with him again, but by dint of great manoeuvring, tact and patience, he managed to persuade her not to come.

'She's going to see the film, 'The Young Winston', instead,' he told me as we drove over the bridge at Newhaven, on the 'heels' of a Fyffes banana van.

'You're very good to her,' I said, as we passed the yellow van.

'I've no choice, I'm always there, I'm a sitting duck, you might say!' But he smiled as he said it, and spoke without rancour. He took that kind of thing in his stride.

There wasn't so much traffic on the road as we had feared, and in no time at all we were approaching Fawding, putting the car on the park. I got out and stretched. I felt light and free. We were a colourful pair this afternoon . . . Duncan in blue cords and a thick white jersey, I in a Black Watch tartan kilt and a bottle green sweater to tone. The kilt was easy to walk in, it swung just above my knees, and the sweater was just right for an autumn day, being tight and warm and long-sleeved, the collar reaching up to my ears.

Duncan was looking at me. I hoped he approved.

'It'll be blowy on top. Are you sure you'll be warm enough?'

'Plenty . . . I hardly ever feel the cold, only when I'm miserable inside.'

'And today you're not?'

'Today I feel fantastic . . . on top of the world!'

'So do I . . . so do I . . . on top of the world!' He kissed me lightly on the tip of my nose and we began the walk through the town.

It was mild for October and almost windless. The sun cast a golden glow. But there was more than a feel of autumn in the air . . . a touch of winter maybe. There were bonfires on the allotments, woodsmoke on the breeze, leaves scattered the streets and the lawns in the gardens. On the cliff-top it was dry, the turf sprung under our shoes; we talked very little as we climbed. And the air was full of noises, mixed bird noises; the gulls wheeled and called, stretching out their necks, putting their legs down straight as they landed, sitting in pairs on the edge. Away on our left was the Fawding golf-course; we could hear the shouts of the players, the click of the ball . . . see the caddies wheeling their trolleys behind.

'What made you suggest we came here today?' I asked, as we got to the top at last, turning round to look at the wide sweep of bay, the little town spreadeagled at our feet. Curving in the distance was the long harbour arm, there was the plume of a steamer coming out.

'It could be our last chance before the rough weather comes. And it was a standing date if you remember, Nina . . . remember that day in the train?'

I did, of course. I remembered all right, yet it seemed a very long time ago. It was the day I'd gone to Fawding and when I got home Charles told me we wouldn't be going to Brighton to live. He'd seemed pleased, I recalled; he hadn't really wanted to go there. Brighton (to Charles) after Norfolk Street, The Strand, would have seemed infra dig, a bit of a *de*-motion. London was the best of all worlds to Charles; he was very much an urban man. Nevertheless we'd come close . . . very close then. And everything had improved . . . for just a little while. And it seemed a long time ago, years and years ago, instead of only just six months.

'I didn't know you then, Duncan, and Leila was so curious, asking me questions, summing me up, frightening me almost to death.'

'You stood up to her well, you don't frighten easily. She wanted to know about you yesterday. She's got it all worked out, thinks we'd make a good pair. She's not against divorce, she says.'

'Most elderly people are . . . against divorce I mean. They think the young are feckless, falling in and out of love, having affairs, sleeping around, casting off lovers like layers of clothes . . . anxious to sample the next.'

'Yet really, by today's standards, we're not all that young . . . twenty-four and twenty-eight . . . we're practically middle-aged!'

'I'd better start looking out for grey hairs and wrinkles!'

'You'd be absolutely gorgeous, even with those.'

We stopped and kissed again. It was really quite hilarious . . . we felt like teenagers on the spree.

We linked hands, turned westwards, walked into the sun. There was a quietness between us now which I didn't want to break . . . didn't want to break the spell. And it *was* rather spell-binding, strolling like this, with the breeze in our ears, ruffling the grass, and below us the hiss of the sea. It was a blue sea today, with a clear-cut horizon, scarcely a cloud in sight.

The cliff jutted, changed colour

— white to cream to terracotta, back to white again. There were long deep chasms, or chines, I think they're called . . . fascinating to look down, the sea seemed miles below, shaped in a kind of 'v'. I knew this was roughly where mother had fallen. Had she slipped here . . . or here . . . or here? It was a long way down, such a long way down. She could have known nothing, practically nothing . . . it would have been over in a flash. Charles was right, I had brooded too much.

'I don't think anyone every really dies,' Duncan's arm drew me back from the edge, 'and I don't mean there are droves of spooky spirits around . . . I just think we're ploughed back into all this . . . into this beauty, this vista, these surrounds. I think we become part of it all.'

'Rather like profits are ploughed back in a business?'

'Something like that perhaps . . . I can't *explain* what I mean . . . it's more of a feeling . . . I feel it when I'm painting. I'm absolutely convinced then that we just *go* on . . . go on in some form, in some kind of way. We're not just extinguished like a flame.'

'I think I know what you mean . . . one does get a feeling . . . especially up here, cut off from the world. Anyway, so far as mother's concerned, I'm over it now. I just can't keep *thinking* any more. But I did think, of course; I thought all the time; but most of all I thought about Charles. I stumbled on a root and Duncan's arm came round me. We began the walk down to Dene Gap.

'I love you, Nina, but you must know that.' We turned and faced each other, the sun in our eyes. His face in this light seemed cast in gold . . . his hair, his forehead, the well-modelled nose. 'I love you, Nina, you must know that.'

Without being conceited I thought that he must. Why else would he have taken the trouble he had with a girl, a married woman who promised him nothing, who gave him nothing but a wary friendship, a reluctant passion tightly bolted back by a conscience the size of a house.

He bent and kissed me . . . differently this time . . . as he had on the pier that day. Once again I was transformed, transported, or both . . . once again I rose up . . . ascended . . . climbed the heights . . . once again it was as if the lid shot off the world, showing me just for a fleeting second what life was all about. I felt then that I loved him and I was tremulously afraid . . . for I knew I didn't want to, I knew it couldn't be. And I think perhaps he knew it too.

We sat down on a seat . . . I leaned against his shoulder. We sat there for a long time not saying anything . . . unable, unwilling perhaps to utter the words that would bring our relationship out in to the open . . . bare it for what it was.

'Do you love me?' he said at last. 'Have I any chance, do you love me?'

I smiled and touched his face; I did

my best to joke.

'You sound like Reb Tevye in 'Fiddler on the Roof'.'

'And like him I want an answer. I'm serious, Nina. For the first time in my life I want a girl for keeps. I want to marry you when you're free.'

'I don't think I know what I feel,' I lied (I was always lying these days, it was becoming quite a habit), 'I don't know what I feel, I can't tell what I feel. I may never fall in love again.'

'But when you're divorced, when you're free . . . '

'I don't know, I can't tell. It's too far in the future, I can't tell now, it's too soon.' I felt desperately unhappy I could hardly frame the words. Perhaps even now I couldn't believe it would happen; divorce . . . Charles and I . . . how *terrible* it was . . . divorce, like adultery was just a word, until it applied to oneself.

'Nina darling . . . listen to me . . . I can wait if I have to.'

There was the faintest emphasis on

the last four words. 'If I have to . . . if I have to . . . I can wait if I have to' . . . I knew what he meant of course. We didn't have to wait, we could start living together; we could start now . . . we didn't have to wait. Surely that was the best thing, surely that was the answer. And yet . . . and yet . . . was it right, would it last? All lovers start well, enchant one another . . . all lovers live in an ivory tower; but for how long, for how long . . . would it last? And if it didn't, what then? What would it make me? Would I just go on like that all my life, having a series of affairs? I knew that I couldn't. I knew that I would not. Yet perhaps . . . with Duncan and I . . .

'I'm afraid to feel again. I just want to shut it out!'

'That's defeatist talk, my dearest . . . those are nonfighter's words.' His fingers traced the line of my jaw.

'I can't fight my way into another marriage, Duncan. Perhaps I love you at this moment . . . perhaps I love you now. But it seems so precarious, so

. . . on the razor's edge. And besides
. . . I'm married to Charles.'

'Spoken with pride, or despair, or a mixture of both?'

I looked at him sharply; he was quick to catch on. His tranquillity was misleading . . . it cloaked unusual depths. He was intuitive, tuned in; he could sense a mood, respect it . . . not ride roughshod or try to change it to his. He'd be marvellous as a lover, why couldn't I settle for that . . . why did I have to keep analysing things . . . why wasn't I sure of myself?

'I suppose I was proud being married to Charles, when I was living with him, I mean. It was a strain keeping up because we were so different, but when I made him proud of me, when it *did* work out, it was a pretty heady feeling, like achieving something great.'

'He was a hard taskmaster, in other words.'

'He expected . . . liked . . . wanted things done well.'

'So your marriage was a series of

jumps for perfection . . . more like an endurance test.'

I was taken aback by his tone. He sounded cross. I tried my best to explain.

'It would have been all right, but there was always Dal. She was right for him, you see.' A wave of desolation drenched me like rain. I shivered as the wind caught my skirt. 'She's always been there in the back of his mind, waiting in the wings, waiting for her cue; I suppose I gave her that when I got disheartened and ceased to try . . . or ceased to try quite hard enough.'

I was crying now, really crying, tear of self-pity. I would really have to take myself in hand.

'Forget him . . . forget him . . . I'd like to kick his teeth in!' Duncan rained kisses on my sopping wet face his voice was urgent in my ear.

'You shouldn't say that. It was my fault too. We were different and I didn't always bother to adjust. I was deliberately perverse and sometimes I was flippant, purposely to make him cross.'

'Marry me . . . marry me . . . when the time comes. And there'll be no adjusting necessary; we suit each other *now*; we're made for each other, don't you feel that . . . you must Nina . . . you must feel it . . . we're two of a kind!'

'Birds of a feather, or like-unto-like?' I could smile again now. That was how I was with Duncan . . . laughing one minute, crying the next . . . emotionally unstable, like balancing on a pin. I'd been that way since the funeral when Charles had told me off . . . 'you can't help, you never could . . . you can't help, you never could'. 'I expect I could help you in all sorts of ways?' I queried now, staring out to sea.

'Help me . . . help me? What a question to ask!' He stroked my hair roughly, tugging it at the crown; he pulled my head backwards, forcing me to look at him, 'I love you, do you hear . . . I love you, Janina . . . I'd be lost without you . . . bereft without you. I feel you belong to me! I can't believe

I'm feeling that all on my own. Surely you feel *something* for me?'

'I must have time to think. I know it sounds dreadful, as though I'm two-timing, but however much I push it out, part of me belongs to Charles. That's not what I want, but it's the way that it *is*. It'll probably always be so.'

He said nothing else. We walked back to Fawding . . . the sun at our backs, our shadows long in the grass. Two separate shadows thrown lengthily forward, then his arm came round me, drawing me close, and the two shadows merged, became one in the grass. Yet was there anything especially significant in that? . . . they were only shadows after all.

We reached the promenade, walked along by the beach huts, turned up into the town.

'Will you think it over, give me an answer, when I get back from Lemston next week?' (Duncan was spending a week at Lemston staying with father and Valerie. I couldn't help wondering how much they knew, or guessed, and what they thought about it all. Father liked Duncan, he was always telling me so. But Valerie was different . . . Duncan was her son.)

'What would your mother say if we ever linked up?'

'She'd be delighted, of course; she'd be tickled pink.'

But it seemed to me his face took on a rather dogged look. And I wondered if Valerie would.

12

On Tuesday night I awoke to the sound of falling rain, not the gale lashed sort that drives like pebbles on the windows, but a strong steady downpour, making a soft insistent 'hush'.

I lay flat on my back. I felt relaxed. I have never minded rain. I have always rather liked it. Some of my happiest moments have been spent on rainy days, so now the sound of it soothed me, I felt I could think.

How was I going to plan my life? Was Duncan the answer? Could I make him happy? Would a marriage between us work? My confidence was low, I was afraid to try again. Yet it would be very easy to agree to marry him, when I was free, I mean. It would be even easier and far less drastic, to simply move in with him in his maisonette near The Lanes. It wouldn't be a hole-in-the-corner affair; it would be open, above-board, nothing underhand. And it would be marvellous not to be alone any more, to have someone coming in each and every night, fulfilling my need to look after a man again; to have someone to think of, someone to be with . . . 'someone to care for, someone to love'. It would be easy, he wanted me, he'd made that very plain. So why did I hesitate, what was I waiting for, and why did I lie here wakeful in the darkness, listening to the sound of the rain?

Tomorrow was Wednesday, the day I didn't work. Duncan was still at Lemston, staying with our parents. How strange it seemed to say that, as though we were related . . . as though we were related, brother and sister, when there was no actual blood tie at all. And how *would* Valerie react to the news that we were attracted, were very much more than 'good friends'. Duncan had made it plain that he intended to forewarn them. 'I shall have to, Nina. They ought to have some inkling. They are our kith and kin, after all.'

No, Duncan would never be underhand. He wasn't that sort of man.

At seven o'clock I got up and made toast and coffee, wondering what to do with my day. Estelle was in Town. She very often was, staying at The Hilton this time. She really was a woman of absolute extremes ... slumming it down here, swanning it up there, with a half-way house establishment at 'Willow Barn' ... a movable feast indeed. What must it be like, going through life like that; unsettling surely, lonely at times. I knew it wouldn't suit me; I wasn't as tough as that ... nor rich enough, nor clever enough ... nor as grabbing and reckless as she. Charles had made a fair assessment of Estelle too ... he'd been right in very many ways.

I thought I'd probably go out into the country, get a Southdown 'bus. I could go inland and walk on my own, try to sort myself out. More rain was forecast, but that wouldn't matter. I'd got a mackintosh and wellington boots; I could tuck my hair under a hat. Estelle had a wide-brimmed yellow wet-look hat. She wouldn't mind me borrowing that.

The 'bus left The Steine at a quarter to one. I managed to get a seat at the front. It was drizzling, misty, grey and uninviting. I wasn't sorry when we turned away from the sea and moved north-easterly inland. The 'bus lumbered along under the scanty-leafed trees, bordering the narrow lanes. We passed through villages with strange-sounding names, tiny thatched cottages, sprawling farm-buildings, black and white cows in the fields. One cow was running in the clumsy way cows have, looking all corners and bones.

After roughly half an hour the 'bus turned yet again, until we were on the main road. And presently it stopped at a grey stone church, in front of an overgrown pond.

Obeying a sudden impulse I got off there, with one or two other mackintoshed people who probably lived nearby. It was a very busy road, and I crossed by a bollard, stepping on to a wide grass verge. Trees flanked this side and as I stepped between them I was instantly curtained off, shut away from the traffic, faced by the rural scene.

I looked about me wondering in which direction to walk. The signpost said 'Mildhayes', I knew this must be Mildhayes church. The vicarage lay alongside, surrounded by hedges, and I remembered reading something in the *Sussex Times* about the vicar being quite a young man. He'd come from a very tough dockside area; was something of an innovation, being rather avant-garde. He was planting bulbs this afternoon, I could see him through the hedge. I was surprised he wore his clerical collar for things like that.

I also remembered reading something about the church; that it was fantastically old; that it was reputed to have been standing there in 1066 when William the Conqueror's invading boats grazed on Mildhayes' sands. It had a Norman tower and a swinging tapsel gate; and again on impulse and to impress the gardening vicar, I passed through the gate and up the stone path and into the ancient porch.

There was a heavy oak door with an iron ring handle. I twisted it, pushed it and stepped inside, careful to close the door quietly behind me, trying not to let it bang.

The church was empty, very small, hollow-sounding; and as the echoes of the closing door faded away, I walked very carefully over the matting on the floor, breathing very shallowly, afraid to make a noise, careful of the rustling of my mack.

It was so *old*. I could sense it, feel it, walk in awe of it; even its smell was old. I was upset, I was *de trop*, I wasn't right for it; I was an intruder here, I didn't fit. I was suddenly thankful I had on

Estelle's hat. It was better to be hatted I felt.

My hand trailed the pew ends as I went up the aisle. They were ice-cold, rock-hard, pitted and stained. In the nave the timbered beams, the wall plates, the struts, added to the feeling of by-gone days, added to the feeling of age.

I sat down in a pew. It was very uncomfortable. I stared at the lectern, at the altar, at the Cross. And as I sat there quietly by myself, as I sat there dreaming, thinking of nothing very much . . . my mind seemed to move from the present-day to the past . . . to that of hundreds of years ago. It was a humbling experience, yet reassuring too. It made such words as 'time', 'past' and 'present' even 'death' seem unimportant, oddly unreal. I felt I knew what Duncan meant up on the Head . . . that we none of us go out like a flame. I sat there for ages. I was stiff when I got up. My boots plopped incongruously on the red matting again, as I made my way back to the door.

The sun was shining now, diffused through the mist. When I opened the door it seemed to settle about me, yellowing my shiny white mack. I still felt bemused, my mind was still way back. I sat down on a bench beside the weedy pond and tried to reorientate myself.

It was then that I saw the man. He was coming through the trees, walking round the pond, walking towards me, moving through the long wet grass to where I sat.

I knew him at once. He was the man who'd been following me up until ten days back. It couldn't have been coincidence that he was here this afternoon. He must have followed me, been somewhere on the 'bus. I felt a tinge of alarm, nothing more than that . . . at least I could solve the mystery now.

'Good afternoon, Miss Cullimore. You won't mind if I join you?'

He sat down on the bench, a fair

distance from me. There was nothing even faintly menacing about his attitude.

'Who are you? What do you want? And how do you know me?'

He smiled, a bland smile, without showing his teeth. He slid up closer on the seat.

'My name's Morrison . . . Alec Morrison. Doesn't that ring a bell?'

He was quite well-spoken . . . there was something odd about him. I felt a desperate unease. 'I don't think so. Should it? Have we met before?' In a kind of stupefaction, almost in disbelief, I watched his hand come down on the hem of my mack as it lay between us on the seat.

Unease quickened to fear. Who was this man. How did he know my name?

He inclined towards me; he had strange light eyes; his mouth was drawn in; there was sweat round his nose. His breath fanned my face . . . I leaned involuntarily backwards. And then he moved . . . snatched my arm . . . his free hand clamped my mouth . . . his legs twisted round mine in a kind of pincer movement . . . I struggled, rocked, pushed against him . . . we toppled off the seat.

We were in the grass now . . . I was fighting for my life . . . we were in the grass now, I knew he meant to kill me. His fingers were steel wires cutting into my throat . . . my neck would break . . . my neck would break . . . I'd die . . . I couldn't scream.

I shall die . . . I shall die . . . I shall die like this. I pushed him with my hands . . . my wrists bent back . . . I shall die . . . I shall die . . . a skidding, slewing blackness. I mustn't . . . I mustn't . . . I can't . . . I can't . . . I won't. Pain slivered through my head . . . amplified his words. I shall die . . . I shall die . . . I mustn't . . . I won't. And his words still kept coming, sliding into my ear. 'I'm Alec Morrison . . . you remember me. I'm Alec Morrison, your father killed my wife, he could have saved her . . . he didn't bother . . . he didn't care . . . he let her die. So I killed your mother . . . revenge is sweet . . . it was easy up there, up there on the cliff . . . she didn't even hear me . . . one push and she was gone. You're like her, aren't you . . . dotes on you, doesn't he . . . your father dotes on you. I knew it was you . . . I saw you in the street. An eye-for-an-eye, Miss Cullimore . . . revenge is sweet . . . dotes on you, doesn't he . . . you can't move, can you . . . you can't shout, can you . . . you're like her, aren't you . . . I knew you at once. And now you're going to join her . . . to join her . . . to join her . . . now you're going to . . . going to . . . going to . . .'

I was fighting for my life, but more feebly now. But I wouldn't die, I wouldn't die . . . I won't . . . I won't . . . I won't . . . trees spinning, earth tilting like a crazy plate. I won't . . . I won't . . . his face was touching mine . . . his breath fanned my mouth . . . for a second he hesitated . . . the tight band eased. I drew my last remaining breath to scream and scream and scream. I rolled face downwards in the grass.

I was in a high, hard bed. There were other beds opposite . . . a strip of highly polished floor. My throat was bandaged, my face felt stiff and sore. It hurt me to breathe or move my arms. There was pain in my chest, my throat was agony . . . the man . . . the grass . . . the trees.

'Where?'

The whiteness beside my bed moved into focus, and I saw it was a nurse of some kind.

'Mildhayes General, Mrs. Redman. You're quite safe now.'

'But . . . '

'You have three fractured ribs and a very bruised throat . . . otherwise no harm done.'

'But what . . . how long . . . '

'You were attacked near Mildhayes church yesterday afternoon. It was an attempt on your life. You were saved by the vicar, who fortunately heard you scream.'

Memory flooded back, was suddenly crystal clear. 'Morrison . . . the man . . . he ought . . . he's dangerous.'

'Now don't try to talk. Morrison is dead. He ran across the road under an articulated lorry. He was alive when he was brought here, made a statement before he died.'

'I must speak to my father. I have to see my father!'

'Later . . . you must try to sleep now.'

Something pricked my arm. I drifted off, I couldn't help it. Someone took my hand. It was a man's, it was lovely. Now I was a balloon floating high in the sky, anchored by the hand that held my string. 'Don't let me go . . . don't let me go. You'll have to hold me very tight in case I float away.'

'You're safe and secure, don't worry, my darling.' The voice seemed to come from very far off. Whose was it? I couldn't tell.

When I next came to father was beside me. His face looked grey and prickly as though he'd not shaved.

Perhaps he'd been there all night.

'Daddie . . . '

'How are you, sweetheart?'

'How did you find out . . . how did you know. And what time is it? How long have I been here?' I was clear-headed lucid and yet I was not. I kept coming and going like the sea. There was a sensation like pain and yet not pain, as though it were being held back.

'You had a letter from me in your handbag. They got on to me straight away.'

'You know about . . . '

'Morrison made a statement. Yes, I know, Nina.' There was a look about him, a shocked look, that I was powerless to dispel. What could I say? What was there to say? What did one say at times like this. I wanted to insist, as he'd insisted years before, that mother could have known nothing . . . it would have been very quick. But I was tired, I couldn't manage it. My throat ached and pulsed. Valerie would help him; Valerie was his . . . Valerie would know what to say and do. Valerie would ease his stress.

'So long as you're all right, Nina . . . so long as you're all right.'

'Someone ought to get in touch with Charles.' I said, just before I drifted off.

$$\star \quad \star \quad \star$$

On the third day they told me I was doing very well, and a policeman came and took some notes. I was still sleeping a lot and not worrying very much. People came and went and said the usual things. Duncan looked ill, I couldn't think why. I tried hard to concentrate on what I should remember, but my thoughts kept rolling away from me like marbles . . . I couldn't seem to catch them up.

Duncan and father were always together, glued together like twins. Estelle came too, blaming herself, saying it was her fault, she should have known the man. I heard father and her discussing it over my bed when they thought I was asleep one day.

'He came to Forge Lane a few weeks back, asking after 'Miss Cullimore'. I *knew* I'd seen his face before, yet I couldn't place it. And of course it was ages ago, all of nine years, just after his wife died when he slung that brick . . . I was staying with you and Mary at the time.'

'He was in a mental hospital for months after that . . . came out presumably cured.'

'Poor Mary . . . my God . . . what a thing to happen! And now Nina . . . after all this time!'

'She's like Mary . . . she just happened to be here . . . he just happened to see her . . . a ghastly sequence of events.'

'Oh, John, if only I'd remembered him, been able to place him. I'm so sorry, I'm so *sorry*, I let the child down. I should have taken care of her. I let her down!'

'No one's let me down . . . you've all been lovely.' I said hazily and drunkenly, opening my eyes, 'I wasn't raped, nor badly hurt, just bashed around a bit. Now could you please all go away.'

Perhaps speaking my mind was a forerunner to improvement, because the next day I was sensible, in control of myself. Dozing after lunch, awoken by the bell (bells and buzzers were always going. It was like being back at school). I saw a different person approaching my bed, someone round and chunky in a light grey suit, someone with a full-blown face.

'Uncle Joce!'

'Janina my dear . . . my very dear girl!' He blew his nose violently, trumpeting like a horse. On my locker lay an outsize bouquet of roses, beribboned and cellophane-wrapped.

'Roses, how lovely! You are good to me!'

'You should be in a private room. I'll see to it at once!' He glared over his shoulder at the bower of plaster legs, suspended by pulleys and cords.

'It's not worth it, Uncle Joce. I'm not badly hurt. My ribs are painful, but they're nothing to worry about. I'm only really in here for shock.'

'You might have been killed.'

'That was the idea!'

'Shocking thing . . . shocking . . . old patient of your father's, getting his own back, I hear?'

'He was nuts, poor man . . . been having treatment for years.'

'Should never have been loose . . . never have been loose!' Uncle Joce seemed jumpy, short of words. Perhaps he hated hospitals, felt uncomfortable in them. He kept fidgeting and fussing, pulling at his ear, jerking his waistcoat down. 'I suppose you're going to marry that young Greek god out there? I suppose he's in the running for your hand?'

'You sound as though you think there might be a queue.'

'Well damn it, you're a very pretty girl.'

'You seem to forget I'm married to Charles. I shall never marry again.'

'Still fond of him, are you?' He was one of those people who avoid the word 'love'.

'Yes.'

'Does he . . . does Charles know?' I asked, trying to sound ordinary. 'Know I'm in here, I mean.'

'I've done my best to contact him . . . so far with no success.'

'But the office?'

'Rudgleys say he's in Toronto, settling Tim's affairs.'

'But surely he left them an address.'

'They say not. It seems he only intends to be away ten days.'

'So he could be home tomorrow, or the day after that?'

'I'll get in touch with him . . . don't you worry . . . I'll see to everything. I'll get him here all right!'

'Don't coerce him, Uncle Joce. He hates being forced.' I was remembering Dallas. Was she with him in Canada? It seemed very likely of course. But somehow I couldn't quite ask about that. I felt I'd rather leave it to chance.

'Leave it to me, my dear. Don't you worry your pretty head!' And he patted me on it with such force and vigour, it was all I could do not to wince. 'And, Janina . . . '

'Yes, Uncle Joce?'

'You're a fine girl . . . a brave one. Whatever happens . . . whatever comes to pass, I think very highly of you, very highly indeed. You're a fine young woman, nothing can alter that.'

He kissed me and puffed off, looking acutely embarrassed. And embarrassment was a new 'coat' for Uncle Joce to wear. I couldn't understand it. I felt disturbed and mystified. I also had the feeling that whatever he'd come to tell me he hadn't managed to get it off his chest.

What it could be I had no idea . . . unless it was something to do with Charles.

★ ★ ★

In the meantime all sorts of arrangements were being made for when I would be discharged. I knew I ought to make a stand, say what *I* wanted to do, but as I still felt rotten and couldn't think ahead, I let them get on with it . . . do what they would.

Father and Valerie were adamant that I went home for a time, home to Lemston to have a good rest and then get a job of a sort. It seemed a reasonable solution . . . I couldn't *keep* staying with Estelle. Perhaps it would be better to settle down in Norfolk. I could even take up medical work again.

'And I could come down for weekends occasionally,' said Duncan, one evening when he came in to see me. There was a question in his eyes and I didn't know how to answer it. I felt badly about it, but I just couldn't bother . . . it was too much effort to reason and why . . . it was too much effort to think.

If only Charles would come . . . only he could settle things. If he saw me, if we saw each other, if he knew I'd nearly been killed . . . wouldn't it do *something* . . . rekindle the spark. Surely it would matter to him just a little bit that I'd very nearly departed this earth.

The vicar had been to see me the day before — the Reverend Donald Chatsworth, who'd come to my rescue . . . knocked Morrison off my chest. He looked young for a vicar, was thickset and jolly, his cheeks shone healthily when he smiled.

'Well, well, well, Mrs. Redman. And how are you today? Not too much the worse for wear, I hope?' He'd brought me some flame chrysanthemums out of the vicarage garden . . . 'August Queen' he told me they were called.

I tried to thank him for what he'd done, but it was really very difficult, practically impossible. How *do* you thank someone for saving your life, particularly a parson who believes in God and love, not fisticuffs and fighting and summoning the police. What I would have liked to have asked him more than anything else was what were his views on married couples . . . what did he think of divorce.

★   ★   ★

Despite the tablets they gave me, I didn't sleep much at night, and it's a strange experience to lie awake in a hospital ward. It's dimly lit, so you can see most of the other beds. There are mutterings and groanings and heavings and creakings. The plaster legs look ghostly like branches of trees, and there is always someone sitting in the middle of the ward, at a desk, or table, under a shaded lamp; she is always very young, a student nurse perhaps. Sometimes another nurse comes through the swing doors and they whisper together softly, sometimes they laugh. I *could* have been a nurse . . . why hadn't I trained as one? Would this be the answer, would I make a good nurse, was I too old to start. A paper bag rustled on the other side of me. It was 'grannie with the femur' tucking into her sweets. The sharp smell of peppermint wafted over my bed. I wasn't tired; I was wide awake. I wished I could get up and walk about as I'd often done at Estelle's when I couldn't sleep.

How would I like living at home with father and Valerie? Valerie, I had to admit, had been very nice about it.

'I'm looking forward to it, Nina. We can get to know each other. It's such a pity we're nearly strangers . . . we ought to get over that.'

I could see now that she was very suitable for father. She was steady, reliable, and he needed that. He needed someone badly to help him in his work, which I knew she did very well. It wouldn't do for me to try and muscle in on that. I'd have to get a job in Lemston or at the hospital in King's Lynn. The prospect didn't depress me, but it didn't enthral me either. If only Charles would come.

He came the next day, out of visiting hours. He came during the morning, after the doctors' round. He came, he said, as soon as he got back . . . as soon as Rudgleys had rung through.

'I was absolutely rocked, Nina. I just couldn't believe it. I should have answered your letter, but I've well . . . there's been so much to get through. And I didn't really think it could be anything serious, about the man following you, I mean.'

'So you didn't reply. You assumed . . . it was nothing?'

'Nina . . . please . . . ' His hand trembled against my face. Oh yes he minded . . . he did mind. Yet when he bent and kissed me I knew.

'It's no good, is it Charles? Even now it's no good?'

He shook his head. 'I'm sorry. I'm just sorry.'

'You're living with Dal?'

'Yes.'

He still held my fingers. I drew them away. 'I tried Nina . . . I did try . . . I *ached* to do the right thing!'

'But it was bigger than both of you!'

'Don't be bitter.'

'But it's her you want?'

'I have to have her.'

'Oh, well that's it then.'

We looked at one another. His expression was kind . . . kind, but determined too. This, then, was the finish, the absolute finale. I knew now how very much I'd pinned my hopes on Charles . . . hoped that we might start again, patch up; compromise, yes, even if we only compromised.

'Darling, you'll fall in love again. You'll meet someone else. You'll marry again . . . some day.'

I looked away, closed my eyes. He could have spared me that. He'd already made his point, he didn't have to hammer it home. He didn't love me, he didn't care, so he could afford to discard me . . . tacitly hand me over to a mythical someone else.

'Thank you for coming, Charles, but feel free to go.'

'I've . . . I've brought you some fruit. I left it with the sister.'

'That's nice.'

'Goodbye then, Nina . . . and . . . and good luck.'

I shut my eyes. I couldn't bear it. I felt him kiss my cheek. When I raised my lids he was walking swiftly up the ward, striding out in the way I remembered so well . . . very upright, very confidently . . . a jaunty set to his head . . . a dark red head with thick springing hair . . . hair that would never properly take a hat . . . hair that was rough to touch.

He reached the swing doors. He pushed his way through them. For a second, a fleeting second, I saw the whole of him there; then he was through and away; they swung to again, as if they had swallowed him up.

And I would never see him again. I would never see him again. I would never, never, ever see him again.

There was movement at my bedside. Someone touched my forehead, felt it clinically, gave a little 'tut'.

'Oh come now, Mrs Redman . . .

come, come, come! That handsome young husband of yours will be back in no time. He'll be back again this evening, you'll see.

I smiled at her rigidly. I felt hollow inside.

I knew that he would not.

★　★　★

I vowed I'd never marry again, but as I've said before . . . time changes things and people, and gradually I changed; or I changed my attitude, I stopped being afraid . . . afraid to love a man again.

Three years almost to the day of that final parting with Charles, I married Duncan in the registry office at Lemston, near King's Lynn, and never has there been a happier bride.

And a great deal happened in our first year of marriage. Duncan sold his business and joined up with his friend at Windsor (still antique renovating, of course, but on a much more interesting scale). Estelle sold us 'Willow Barn';

274

she was tired of it, she said; Duncan and I could hardly believe our good luck.

But the most wonderful thing of all is our two-month-old son. His name is Simon and he's perfect . . . big and blond and beautiful. He's got his father's placid temperament too.

It's autumn again now, and we're strolling in the garden. It's evening and the shadows are long. The river is quiet, dark and mysterious; the willows are motionless, the ducks settle for the night. In the orchard the trees hang heavy with fruit; it's been a good plum crop, the apples come next; soon I shall be bottling, and making pounds and pounds of jam. Duncan has a very sweet tooth.

My hand lies in his as we walk back to the house. I am happy, entirely content.

But I shall never forget Charles. That would be impossible. I no longer love him . . . I think of him very little; yet there are times, sometimes when the memory of him is strong, fanned to life perhaps by a scent, a feeling, a tune. For instance now as we climb the veranda steps, scraping the mud off our shoes . . . from way upstream (maybe sung by a rowing eight) comes the strains of the Eton Boating Song . . . clearly over the water.

And for a second, just a second, my mind goes back . . . to when I was married to Charles.

THE END

THE BOYS NEXT DOOR

Janet Chamberlain

When Ross Anderson and his lively nephews move in next door to Alison Grainger, it ends her well-ordered life — a life that doesn't include children. The noise is bad enough, but Alison becomes critical of Ross's method of childcare even as she becomes attracted to him. She becomes involved in their welfare despite herself. But when it emerges that the boys' grandmother has persuaded Alison to record Ross's progress with the children, the rift between them gets even bigger.

WHITE LACE

Rosemary A. Smith

Dismissed from her employment at the academy, the future seems bleak for Barbara Thorpe. But a whirlwind romance leads to marriage when she meets Kieran Alexander. However, upon being taken to his home, Rowan Castle, she is overawed by its grandness. Barbara is further disquieted by the fact that she knows nothing about him, and by meeting the beautiful but arrogant Kerensa Templeton. First her marriage, then her life, will be threatened before she can discover both the truth and real happiness . . .

CAMPAIGN FOR LOVE

Ginny Swart

Andrea Ross is an artist in the studio of an advertising agency and for a long time she's been in love with dashing Grant Carter, an accounts executive at a rival company. Then the new art director from America, charming, untidy, critical Luke Sullivan turns her working world upside down — along with her heart. But Luke has demons that haunt him from the past, as well as a string of other women in his life.

THE PEBBLE BANK

Sheila Spencer-Smith

Cara Karrivick and her twin sister never knew they had any family on their father's side. But when Cara and Arlene inherit their grandparents' cottage in Polmerrick, Cara visits the house and is delighted when she uncovers so many family secrets. She meets the rather hostile Josh Pellew, but it doesn't spoil her dream of living there. However, as Cara discovers her grandmother's family record, disaster strikes. Can Josh be the one to help her to realise her dream?